CW00589705

BOSS DADDY

A DADDIES INC NOVEL

LUCKY MOON

KEEP IN TOUCH

———————

Thanks for stopping by!

If you want to keep in touch and even receive a naughty little FREE STORY as a thank you for signing up, just head to the link here:

http://eepurl.com/gYVLJ1

As well as keeping you informed of new releases, I'll send you EXCLUSIVE CONTENT, plus COMPETITIONS and polls and lots of other FUN and games.

Also, you can get in touch with me at luckymoonromance@gmail.com or find me on Facebook. I love hearing from fans!

Lucky x

Table of Contents

CHAPTER 1 - DAISY

"Stop it, stop it, stoooooopppppp iiiiiiitttttt!" Daisy screamed into a pillow.

Daisy Grove was a sunshine person. She had the biggest smile of anyone she knew. She wore a ton of yellow—like, a ton. She loved playing games, and singing songs, and pouring glitter on literally *everything*. She even lived, believe it or not, in a place called Sunshine Trailer Park.

But Sunshine Trailer Park had not lived up to its name. And with every day that passed, Daisy found it harder and harder to cling to her sunny personality.

It was difficult to put her finger on exactly what she hated most about this place. Was it the fact that a bunch of the trailers had no restrooms and the residents were dumping their waste into the river? Was it the back-alley drug deals, or the fights she heard in the middle of the night? Was it the old syringes, or the rusty nails in the kids' park across the road?

Actually, no. It was none of those things.

What she hated most of all was the man in the trailer opposite hers. Because morning to night, no matter what, he was *laughing*. Not a light chuckle. Not even a deep belly laugh. No, siree. It was an oddly high-pitched, creepy laugh, occasionally accompanied by horrible, scary smashing sounds. She had no idea what he was smashing in there—plates, glasses, bones?

For the first time in her life, Daisy's sunshine was starting to disappear.

"I never want to hear anyone laugh ever again," Daisy told her pillow. She'd yelled into her pillowcase so much tonight that it was covered in spittle. Oops.

The pillowcase was very special to Daisy. She'd had it since she was a kid. It was a *Cinderella* pillowcase. Daisy loved that movie. The original version from 1950 was the best, of course. Daisy loved to escape through the things she watched on the screen. She'd watch just about anything, but Disney movies

5

were her favorite. And *Cinderella* was the pinnacle, because it reminded her so much of herself.

"I wish you could save me right now, Fairy Godmother," she said to her pillowcase, gazing at the picture of the Fairy Godmother on it. She was waving her wand, and underneath her, it said: "Bibbity-bobbity-boo!" She looked so warm and friendly. Exactly the kind of person Daisy wished she had in her life for real.

Well, she had her best friends, Kiera and Peach, obviously. But she was kinda running away from them right now, so they didn't really count.

Daisy slowed down her breathing, trying to de-stress. She grabbed her cup of coffee off the bedside table. It was starting to go cold, but she didn't care. She took a big swig. Coffee was her main comfort in the trailer. Her tap water tasted disgusting unless you did something to hide it. So, she had a bucket of instant coffee grounds. Plus, she had insomnia. The combination went together perfectly, it turned out.

The creepy man hadn't laughed for thirty seconds or so. Maybe he'd never laugh again. Maybe he'd fallen asleep, or stopped seeing the funny side of things, or—

HahahahaHAHAHAHAHAAAAAAAAAA.

Nope. There it was again, as loud and as amused as ever.

"I need to distract myself," Daisy told her Fairy Godmother. "I could put on my headphones, do some coloring, maybe even get into Little Space—"

It was no use, of course. She'd been here for ten days, and she hadn't managed to get into Little Space once. She was too busy fearing for her own life.

There was a sudden shout outside, then a loud bang as a door slammed shut. Daisy felt her flimsy trailer shake with the vibrations. She peered out the window, wondering which resident it was tonight. The crack dealer with the swastika tattoo? The kid who punched holes in *everything*? The prostitute who looked so young Daisy felt sure she had barely left school?

Ugh. This place. These people. They needed help. Medical, financial, emotional. Unfortunately, Daisy wasn't the person to help them. She'd spent too many years looking after someone else. This was supposed to be the time she started looking after herself.

"I need to get outta here," she told her pillowcase.

She knew that doing some coloring with her headphones on wouldn't work. For starters, her headphones didn't even begin to drown out the sounds around her. She didn't feel comfortable blocking out the sounds, either. She liked to have her wits about her, to be able to listen out for danger. For that reason, she always slept with her shoes on, ready to run at a moment's notice.

She heard the door slam again and looked outside. It was the trailer opposite hers. The laughing man's trailer. Only it wasn't the laughing man charging out of there. It was his wife. Daisy had seen her in the window a couple times, but she'd never seen her leave the trailer before. She was wearing a ripped sweater and nothing but panties on the bottom half. There were bruises on her legs.

Then she saw *him*. The laughing man, staring out the window at the woman. And, of course, laughing. It was strange to see him for the first time. She'd expected a ghoulish figure. A man with one eye, or a giant scar, or red eyes. But the man at the window seemed...ordinary. Normal height, normal build, dull brown hair. Nothing was remarkable, except the laughter that never stopped pouring from his throat.

Daisy wondered whether she should see if the woman needed help. If she needed Daisy to call the police. But she just couldn't bring herself to interfere. She didn't want to put herself in any more danger than she was already in. She hated confrontation. Always had. She would put up with just about anything if it meant she didn't have to confront anyone.

Plus, she was wearing *Cinderella* pajamas. They were yellow and frilly and very much not suited to walking around the trailer park at seven in the evening. Her big, thick-framed yellow glasses drew enough stares as it was. Daisy had been bullied for wearing glasses as a kid, and ever since, she'd tried to show the bullies she didn't care by finding the brightest, most garish spectacles she could.

Normally, Daisy stayed in after seven. She didn't like to wander around outside when it got too late. But honestly, it didn't feel much safer in here. So, why not?

"Right, that's it. Executive decision," she said aloud, pacing up and down the tiny space inside her trailer. "I'm going out."

She downed the rest of her coffee then swapped her pajamas for something a little more...sober. Or, at least, as sober as Daisy's wardrobe allowed her to be. A yellow crop-top and leggings, with a long brown coat she'd bought from a thrift store to try to camouflage herself. The coat was ugly as heck, but at least it meant that people didn't take much notice of her.

"These aren't ideal, though," she said to herself, pulling on her silver, glittery sneakers. They hadn't been glittery when she'd bought them, but she'd soon fixed that.

She made a mental note to buy some more serious-looking shoes from the thrift store. And some more serious-looking clothes. She needed to be able to fade into the background completely. At least she'd stopped smiling at everyone. She'd smiled at people when she had first arrived here, and that led to not one but three men propositioning her, and a woman telling her to "go suck an egg."

When she was ready, she took her *Cinderella* pillowcase off her pillow and stuffed it in her pocket. She could stand just about anything else getting stolen, but not that. That was her lifeline.

She locked her door, and then, keeping her head down and her pace quick, she left the trailer park.

It was always a relief to get out. And a double-relief to make it out in one piece. That place had seriously mis-sold itself on its website where it had described the trailer park as "cozy." Said it was full of "community spirit" and "vintage living accommodation."

Ugh. She was sure there were some decent trailer parks out there. In fact, she'd always found the idea of them to be quite romantic. Like being permanently on vacation in a little cabin.

Never mind.

She'd paid three months' rent upfront, and she couldn't afford to switch places now.

She hopped on a bus and headed for Miami Beach. She loved going there. It always made her feel like a celebrity. The palm-tree-lined streets. The ocean. The bars. The whole reason she'd come to Miami was because she'd heard about a particular bar on Dade Boulevard, but it only opened at seven o'clock, and so far, she hadn't dared to go out at night. Now, finally, she was doing it.

"Oh my goodness, oh my goodness," she said under her breath. "There it is!"

She practically jumped off the bus when she saw it. It was the bar she'd read about on DDlg forums back when she lived in Connecticut. The reason she'd chosen t to live here over any other place in the world: *Dade-D Bar*. It was a play on words for those in the know. Dade-D sounded a bit like Daddy. Or, if you looked at the initials, DD, it made you think of Daddy Dom. Or, at least, it made *Littles* think of Daddy Doms.

It was a dry bar, which kept a lot of the wrong clientèle out. But also, the way that it looked outside told you that this was no ordinary establishment. It had a candy cane porch. A cute little star design over the door. Frosting shaped like teddy bears on the windows.

Of course, it was for strictly over twenty-ones only. But, since Daisy was twenty-three, she was not just allowed in there, she was their *exact* target audience.

"Come on, Daisy. You got this," she said to herself. She'd been through so much lately that it was hard to feel like she belonged here, but she did. She really, really did. She gripped the scrunched-up pillowcase in her pocket for luck.

And the moment she stepped through the door, all her troubles melted away. In less than ten seconds flat, her entire being had filled with sunshine again.

She loved it all. The oversized rainbow-colored tables and chairs. And the picture book corner to her left. And the playpen full of toys on her right. And all the happy, cute, sweet Littles, playing and laughing and having a good time. And, and, and!

She was in heaven.

She looked up at a huge sign displaying more milkshake flavors than she had ever seen in her whole life.

"Okay, Fairy Godmother," she whispered in the vague direction of her pocket. "Looks like we just came home." She could *feel* it. This place was going to be a turning point for her. She'd hear about some amazing new job here. She'd try to make some new friends. She'd finally just be able to be her happy self with no obstacles. She strode up to the bar, and the server gave her the warmest, most genuine smile she'd seen in days.

"Well, hello there, Little one," the server said kindly. Her hair was scraped back in a brown bun and she wore a neat white apron. It could have been the effect that this place was having on Daisy's psyche, but she looked...motherly. "What can I get for you?"

Daisy giggled. She pushed her yellow glasses farther up the bridge of her nose—out of habit rather than necessity—and scanned the list of drinks. She picked out words like "Oreo", "whipped cream", and "gummy sharks."

"Um," she said shyly. "I'd like one of everything, please. No, make that two of everything!"

The woman behind the bar waggled her finger. "You know what, young lady? You look like you need something real special tonight. How about I get you a Daddy's Night Off?"

Daisy's eyes widened. "What's that?"

"Hmmm, let's see..." said the woman, counting ingredients on her fingers as she named them. "There's S'mores, chocolate chips, cookie dough, Cheerios, coconut cream, pretzels, Fruity Pebbles, cotton candy, a cupcake, milk, and...am I forgetting anything?" She paused. "Oh yes, edible glitter."

Daisy grinned from ear-to-ear. "Yes, please. I'll take two. And maybe we could throw a bit of caffeine into the mix? I've not been sleeping too well lately, and I'm kinda wiped out. I haven't managed to get my sixth cup yet today—"

"Let's start you off with just *one* milkshake," said the woman, chuckling and shaking her head. "It's probably got enough sugar in it to last you until at least next Tuesday. As for the caffeine, you really shouldn't be drinking that in the evening, sweetie. It's no wonder you can't sleep. You may as well be trying to sleep upside down."

"I'm not a bat." Daisy snickered. This was the most fun she'd had in forever.

"You most certainly are not," the bartender agreed. "You're a young lady who needs to have a yummy treat, and then get her beauty sleep."

"You give very good advice," Daisy said gratefully. "Who needs a Daddy, eh?"

She wouldn't normally admit to someone in a place like this that she didn't have a Daddy yet. That said, she'd never been in a place like this before. And out there, in the real world, she didn't even admit to being a *Little*. Only her best friends knew that about her. And her ex-boyfriend, of course, but he'd never been her Daddy. Not even close.

"You okay, Little one?" asked the woman. "You're looking kinda glum for someone that's about to get the most decadent freakshake of all time."

"Oops!" Daisy giggled. "Had a bit of a weird month. It's all better now that I'm here, though." Her mouth started to water as she looked at the woman pile scoops of sticky, sugary deliciousness one on top of the other.

"You want to talk about it, sweetie?"

Daisy considered this. She glanced briefly down at her brown coat, thinking about all the things that had been weighing her down lately. She shrugged off the coat and hung it on a peg under the bar, then she shook her head. "I actually think I just want to focus on enjoying myself."

She took a sip of her milkshake, which happened to be the yummiest, most scrumptious drink she had ever put into her mouth. Then, she let out a long, satisfied sigh. That was good. She had to keep the sunshine where it belonged. Eff the trailer park and the creepy laughing man. Eff the good-for-nothing ex and all the problems she'd run away from. All that mattered was *now*! This present moment! Life was good!

Nothing could ever ruin her life again!

Just then, three men walked into the bar. They looked kinda...different than everyone else in here. They were wearing drab business suits and they looked like three of the grumpiest grumps in the history of grumpy grumps. There was no way that these three men were Daddies. More like...*baddies*.

Daisy laughed to herself at her own private joke. She slurped up more of her milkshake, then left it on the bar while she wandered off to check out the toys. She didn't really want to sit at the bar while the three grumps ordered their drinks. She'd just gotten her sunshine back, and there was no way she was losing it, ever, ever again.

"They're dropping like flies," said one of the men gruffly.

"Don't you think I fucking know that?" answered a second moodily.

"Watch your damn language," admonished the third.

Daisy wasn't trying to eavesdrop, but the men all had such deep, booming voices and strangely commanding presences that it was hard to ignore them.

The man who'd spoken last wore a brown waistcoat with a gold chain in the pocket. His shirt sleeves were rolled up, revealing tan arms, and he had a thick silver beard. He reminded Daisy of Pierce Brosnan in the Western drama *The Son*.

Then there was the "dropping like flies" guy. He wore a gray flannel suit with leather patches on the elbows, silver aviator spectacles, and a bow tie. He was the spitting image of Harrison Ford as Indiana Jones when he was in full-on professor mode. Kinda nerdy, but definitely not Indiana Jones in his running-away-from-giant-boulders mode.

And then there was the man who'd used the f-word. He stood front and center at the bar. He wore a dark blue suit, the color of a stormy sky. His hair was flecked with gray and he wore an expensive watch. Who did he make Daisy think of? Hmmm. Oh yes! He had an air of Don Draper from *Mad Men* about him. In both a bad way *and* a good way...

Daisy forced herself to stop staring at them, distracting herself by straightening up the toys in the playpen and arranging them in rainbow color order. She wasn't anal about cleaning or anything–she just enjoyed making things look like rainbows.

"Well, what are you going to do about it?" the Pierce Brosnan lookalike asked Don Draper.

"Why does it have to be me?" Don asked moodily.

"Because you run the damn joint!" said Pierce.

"We're equal owners," Don snapped.

"I'm the behind-the scenes guy," said Harrison Ford. He seemed like the least scary out of the three of them.

"And I deal with the *companies*, not the employees," said Pierce.

Don looked around in frustration. "Where's Tracy? She should be out here."

Daisy noticed that the server, presumably named Tracy, must have popped away from the bar for a moment. As she looked toward the bar, Don Draper caught her eye, and suddenly he clicked his fingers. "Ah, there you are. You must be new. Come on then, Little one. Come here."

Daisy blushed. Little one? Was he being rude? Or hitting on her? Surely not. Did he genuinely think she worked here? She looked around, hoping the real server would come back.

"Don't just stand there gawping at us," he said. "Get here right now, or your ass is on the line."

Daisy's spine stiffened. She didn't like the sound of that. She hated getting in trouble. She was a *good* Little. Always tried her best. Tried to be friendly, tried to be good, tried to be sweet. Tried to be sunshine and rainbows, no matter what.

"Yes, sir," she found herself saying. She scurried over to the bar and hesitated there for a moment.

"Don't you need to go *behind* the bar to serve us?" asked Harrison Ford.

"Um..." Daisy stalled. She glanced over at her milkshake, which was starting to melt down the side of the glass.

"Quit fooling around," barked Don.

Daisy bowed her head. She hated confrontation. "I...Yep. Okay, then." She swallowed, walking nervously through the opening in the bar. This was so very wrong, and yet her feet couldn't seem to stop walking in the wrong direction. "So...what can I get you?" Her voice was shaking. She was going to get in big trouble for this. Big, big trouble.

"Three Cokes," said Pierce. He gestured at Don. "Don't put any ice in *his*. He's cold enough already."

"I'm only cold when staff members let me down," Don replied.

Daisy gingerly took three Coca-Colas out of the fridge and removed the lids using the bottle opener on the bar. She poured them into three glasses, only putting ice in two. There. That wasn't too hard.

Maybe this would help her get a job here? The server would see her any minute and ask her to take the role full-time. She clearly needed a hand. Maybe this was fate! Or...maybe not, since she'd just done something completely illegal.

"Well, who are we gonna get to fill the position, then?" asked Harrison. "Daddies Inc. has gone through three copywriters in the last six months alone."

Daisy's ears perked up. These needed a copywriter? She wasn't *technically* a copywriter, but it was definitely a job she felt she could do. She'd done enough of her ex's writing to know the basics, right? It was good to put herself out there, to go for as many jobs as she could. If there were no openings here at the bar, then she needed a backup plan, right? She only had a week's worth of money left.

She cleared her throat. The instant the three men turned to look at her, she crumbled. Her voice came out tiny and pathetic. "I'm a copywriter."

Harrison Ford leaned in toward her. "You may be a copywriter. But are you a quitter?"

"No," she lied again. "Never quit on anyone in my life."

Except my stepmother, but she was mean.

And my best friends, but they were overprotective.

And my engagement, but that was...a living hell.

Just then, Tracy returned. "Hey, what are you doing standing there?"

Daisy startled like a rabbit in headlights. "I...these guys wanted me to...I'm sorry."

"Get out," she said, her hands on her hips. "And don't come back here again."

Daisy felt her eyes prick with tears. *Oh no.* This place was the whole reason she'd come to Miami. The whole reason she'd been putting up with the trailer park. The whole reason her life was such a mess.

"Of course, ma'am," she said submissively. "I'm so, so sorry. Again."

She grabbed her coat, putting it on and feeling instantly weighed down by its drabness once more. She wanted to say something else–to the server, or to the three men who were staring at her, their faces so disapproving now–but she couldn't speak. There was nothing to say except sorry, a million times over.

"I'm so stupid, Fairy Godmother," she said under her breath as she scurried, shame-faced, out of the bar. "What on earth is my big plan now?"

CHAPTER 2 - MONTAGUE

Montague Manners was pissed off. Granted, he was always pissed off, but today he was *even more* pissed off than usual.

It wasn't just the fact that his copywriter had quit on him this morning. It was...everything. The fact that nothing he ate tasted good anymore. The fact that everywhere he went, the world had a way of letting him down. The fact that everyone always wanted something from him and he was tired of giving it to them.

Damn, he needed a vacation. Although *that* would most likely be a disappointment too.

What he had just seen here, though, at the bar, was the most irritating thing of all. A girl pretending to be a server who was actually a copywriter. He hated when things weren't straightforward. Such a waste of headspace. Waste of time. It confirmed what he already knew: he was right to be wary of strangers.

Bastion elbowed him. "What the hell was that? Should we call the police?"

"Don't be ridiculous," he snapped. "She's a Little. She's probably too submissive to tell us she didn't work here."

"I guess we *are* quite intimidating," Isaac said.

Montague gritted his teeth together. "Not with that bow tie you're not."

"Hey, this is a family heirloom!" Isaac protested.

Tracy, the server, coughed. "Hello? Guys? I know you three are, like, the head honchos here or whatever, but you could have stood up for me."

Montague turned around to look at Tracy. He wasn't too pleased with how she'd handled that, to be honest. *He* was the one who got to decide whether to tell people to take a hike and never come back. Tracy might have managed the bar for the last three years, but she wasn't the boss. *He* was.

"I'm leaving," he told his colleagues brusquely, and he started walking out of the bar.

"Wait!" Bastion called, pulling out his gold pocket watch. "I have a meeting with a client in an hour. We need to talk about this mess with the copywriter *now*."

"No, we don't," Montague huffed, swiftly exiting the bar. "Because there is no mess."

He looked from left to right as he left the bar, trying to spot a brown coat. She couldn't have gotten too far.

And he was right. She was crouching next to a trash can a little way down the sidewalk, with her head in her hands. If he'd been a nicer man, he might have felt sympathy for her. But he wasn't a nicer man.

"Hey," he called out.

She almost jumped out of her skin at the sound of his voice. Oops. Even when he wasn't trying to sound stern, he did.

"I'm so sorry, sir," she said, standing up. "I really didn't mean—"

Now that he was out in the evening sun with her, he noticed that she had a little chocolate around her mouth. He couldn't deny it—that was kinda cute. He wasn't a nice man, no, but he was still allowed to find things cute from time to time.

"I'm assuming you're a Little," he began.

She bit her lip, blushing. That was cute, too. He really had to stop noticing how cute this girl was. Those big, innocent blue eyes framed by those bold, yellow glasses. The blue and yellow reminded him of his favorite candy as a kid: Dubble Bubble. That was weird. He hadn't thought about that gum in years.

"No, sir," the girl said quickly. "I'm not a Little. I'm...I'm...I'm Daisy."

"Well, Daisy," Montague replied. "It's very strange that you were in a bar for Littles and that you dress very much like a Little—" He paused, looking at her awful, unfashionable brown coat. "Apart from that thing." He didn't even try to hide the look of displeasure on his face.

"I was just...you know, exploring the city. I'm so sorry I caused so much trouble. I really didn't mean to—"

"I haven't got time for this," Montague replied curtly. "I can see that you're sorry. And I know that if you *were* a Little, it would have at least explained your submissiveness when we asked you to serve us back there."

Daisy looked as though she was wrestling with something.

"Listen," Montague said, "I didn't come out here to make small-talk. I'm about as uninterested in making new friends as it's possible to be. But you told us back there that you're a copywriter. Correct?"

"Uh, correct," Daisy replied warily.

"I need that position at work filled *pronto*."

"Oh! I see..."

"I'm not really interested in going through the rigmarole of having yet another hiring process. My HR guy isn't too pleased with me right now—lots of hirings and firings lately. But that's another story. Just... bring your resumé to my office tomorrow. Understood?"

"Yes, sir," Daisy said. She even did a little curtsy for him, which was ridiculous. It did help cement his belief that she was a Little, though.

"Oh, and Daisy?" he said sternly. "No more lies. Okay?"

She blushed redder than ever. "No, sir."

Montague nodded, satisfied, then turned on his heel and headed for his beloved Bentley.

The Bentley wasn't his newest car, or even his most expensive one, but he'd always had a soft spot for it. The beluga-colored bodywork. "Beluga" was a fancy way of saying black. The silver seat piping, and the commemorative plaque fitted to the engine, signed by the Chief Executive of Bentley himself. God, it was a beautiful car. Was it a bad sign that his car was pretty much the only thing that made him happy these days?

"What the hell is this?" Montague snapped at his PA, Linda.

Linda lingered anxiously in the doorway. "It's a tall, half-caff, soy latte at a hundred-twenty degrees."

Montague peered at it. "It's the wrong shade. That's cashew milk."

"No, it can't be," Linda replied. "I made it myself, using the machine just like you showed me. I'd never give you cashew milk with your nut allergy."

"It's a *tree nut* allergy," Montague said, somewhat pedantically. "No almonds, no Brazil nuts, no chestnuts, no macadamia nuts, no pecans, no walnuts, and no goddamn cashew nuts."

"I'm sorry, sir," said Linda. "Are you sure it's—"

Montague wasn't going to risk sipping his drink to prove his point. His nut allergy was pretty bad. Not bad enough that he couldn't be in a room with a nut, but certainly bad enough that he couldn't drink the damn things mashed into a cup. Bad enough that he carried around an EpiPen in his pocket wherever he went, just in case.

"Linda, do you remember what could happen to me if I consume tree nuts? Would you like the list again?"

"Not really, sir. I remem—"

"Abdominal camps, vomiting, difficulty swallowing, shortness of breath, anaphylaxis."

"You forgot diarrhea, sir."

Montague narrowed his eyes at her. "I have a meeting in ten minutes. Are you trying to kill me before my meeting?"

Linda's jaw dropped. "No, sir! With all due respect, sir, I've worked here ever since this company began, and I'd never, ever—"

He cut over her voice, rising with indignation. "If you didn't do it on purpose, then I'm not very reassured that you're slipping up, Linda. How old are you now? Sixty? Sixty-five?"

Linda didn't look happy to have been asked that question.

Montague didn't get it. Why did everyone seem to have a problem with how direct he was? It was so much better to cut the crap. Skip all the bullshit, fake flattery and pointless chitchat and talk to people about what you *really* thought and felt. It made everything so much quicker and easier.

"I hope you're not insinuating that I'm ready for an early retirement," said

Linda grumpily, pulling her diamond-knit cardigan over her ample, sagging bosom. "I have years left in me yet."

"Not if you go around poisoning people," Montague snapped, shaking his head. "You know, you should really know better, Linda. Safety is the number one thing in our line of work. I guess not everyone has the same high standards that I do."

"But I *do*, sir," Linda protested. "It's the first time I've slipped up in the full six years that I've—"

Montague raised his palm in the air. "I don't want to hear it, Linda. I have places to go. People to see. Take this out of my sight." He thrust the full coffee cup toward her. "Now go."

Linda mumbled something unhappily, and then left the office.

Montague got up from his desk and walked over to his office window, looking out at the long stretch of sandy white beach and the palm trees and all the people just enjoying life. That used to be him. He wondered if he'd ever get back to that again.

His intercom buzzed, interrupting his reverie, and Linda's voice came through the speaker, tiny and sadder than ever. "It's time for your meeting now, sir."

He was too annoyed with Linda to thank her for the update, especially since he'd literally just mentioned the meeting to her, which meant he clearly remembered it. It was a good thing he wasn't being rushed to the hospital right now. Linda could have done some serious damage with that nut milk. What was all the point of all this hard work if it could just blow up in his face over something so stupid as a damn *nut*?

He walked to the meeting room without bothering to return the greetings of any of his staff members. They knew he wasn't a talkative sort of guy, so it's not like they'd be offended by it. When he arrived at the meeting room, he acknowledged Bastion and Isaac with a nod of the head, as well as Sam, his head of HR. They all nodded back at him, but none of them looked too pleased.

When everyone was present, Sam stood up. He was still quite young in the company, promoted into a powerful role a little sooner than perhaps he'd been expecting. But the truth was, he got things done, and he never fucked up, and that was good enough for Montague.

Sam cleared his throat and pushed a button on a laptop at the front of the room. A graph appeared on the screen. The line was going up toward the top-right corner of the screen.

"Daddies Inc is doing better than ever," he said, pointing at the line. "More investors, more attention, more income, more customer satisfaction." He paused. "But there's a problem." He pushed a button on his keyboard again and the graph changed. This time, the line on the graph was going down toward the bottom right-hand corner of the screen. He pointed at it. "Staff morale."

Montague noticed some members of the boardroom shifting uncomfortably in their seats.

"Can anyone think why morale has been so low here recently?" Sam asked.

"Are the seats uncomfortable?" Montague suggested, looking at them all fidgeting.

"No," replied Bastian coldly. "Look a little closer to home."

Montague was confused. "Are you saying it's *my* seat that's uncomfortable? It seems just fine to me, although I prefer the one in my office —"

"*No*," said Bastian firmly. Then, he turned to Sam. "Why don't you enlighten us, Samuel?"

"Well," said Sam, wringing his hands a little. "There's been a very high staff turnover here lately. Though...whether that's a cause, or a symptom—"

"Stop talking in riddles, man," Montague ordered, standing up. "This isn't like you, Sam. What's the problem? Give it to me straight."

"I think," Sam said, taking a deep breath, "that the staff are starting to feel like there's an issue with the...work environment."

Montague looked at Isaac, who looked away. He didn't bother looking at Bastian. Bastian was clearly shooting him daggers, as usual.

"If you think there's a problem, Sam, sort it out," said Montague. "It really can't be that difficul—"

"I can't, sir. Not unless we commit to making some complete changes at every level of—"

"Is this all I'm going to get from you today?" barked Montague. "Business jargon? I really can't be dealing with this. I have things to do. Important things."

Without giving Sam the chance to reply, he stormed out of the meeting room, feeling even worse than when he'd gone in there. The black cloud over his head just seemed to be growing and growing. It was so big he could actually *feel* it now. Thick, black, and suffocating.

"Sir?"

He heard a familiar voice. Sweet as sugar. Like Dubble Bubble candy. He turned around. Daisy.

"You came," he acknowledged gruffly.

"Yes, sir," she said shyly. He noticed that she was wearing the exact same outfit as yesterday: shitty brown overcoat and all. "Of course I did, sir. It's too good an opportunity to miss, sir."

He noticed that she was clutching a piece of paper with bubbly, babyish handwriting all over it. Plus...was that glitter? Surely that wasn't her resumé?

Linda called from behind her desk. "Do you think you might see her now? She's been waiting for over an hour, sir."

Montague prickled with irritation. Why didn't Linda tell him Daisy was waiting before his meeting? Another black mark next to her name.

"Not my problem," replied Montague abruptly, not even deigning to look in Linda's direction. "I'm a busy man."

"That's why I try to only bother you with one thing at a time," Linda told him with a shrug. "If I'd mentioned our visitor before your meeting, you'd have only gotten worked up."

Montague tried to resist the urge to make a nasty retort. Linda was always thinking outside the box. Making her own decisions about things. He didn't like it. It was not what he wanted in a PA.

Linda leaned over her desk and whispered to Daisy. "It's okay, sweetie.

He'll see you now. Some things are worth waiting for."

CHAPTER 3 - DAISY

_____

Some things are worth waiting for.

The words rattled around in Daisy's head. She felt like she'd spent her whole life waiting. Waiting for her mom to get better when she'd had cancer (she didn't get better). Waiting for her dad to leave her wicked stepmom (he *did* leave, but he left Daisy with the aforementioned wicked stepmom). Then, more recently, she spent six years waiting for her ex-fiancé

to get his act together, hoping that he'd change. Hoping that she'd just wake up one day and there'd be fireworks and a horse-drawn carriage and a happy ever after.

But he didn't change, and nor did their relationship.

Although there was still that nagging little voice inside of her that wondered if she'd just waited a little bit longer, maybe things would've worked out in the end.

That was the problem with being a sunshine person. It was good to always try to look on the bright side, but if you were *too* optimistic, then you just spent your life waiting around for things that never materialized.

Anyway. She was here now, being independent in Miami. No nasty stepmother. No lazy ex. No meddling friends. She was making a life for herself. And part of that involved having to suck up to a nasty, smugly handsome man like Montague Manners. A man who, ironically it seemed, had no manners at all.

When he'd followed her out of the bar yesterday, she'd been shocked and confused. And when he'd started interrogating her about being a Little, she'd panicked. It didn't seem right to confess something so private to a man she barely knew. Besides, he clearly wasn't a Daddy Dom. Maybe a Dom, but definitely not a Daddy. He was much too much of a meanie for that. So, chances were, he would have judged her if she'd told him.

25

As for the copywriter lie...well, she could hardly have backpedaled on that one, could she? She'd told everyone in the bar that she was a copywriter. It didn't feel great to admit that she was being deceitful about that, too.

So, here she was. Attempting to get a job with a handwritten resumé and no experience working as a copywriter whatsoever.

"Well?" Montague barked. "My time is precious."

Your time is precious. *Your* time. Imagine being so rich and successful that you feel like you own time.

She followed him into his office, clutching her piece of paper with trembling hands. She knew that what was written on it was useless. She might have lied about being a copywriter, but she wasn't the sort of person who could just lie about anything and everything. She'd written the truth on this piece of paper. She'd just...embellished it a bit. Didn't everyone do that on their resumés?

The moment she stepped into Montague's office, she almost stepped right out again. It. Was. Ludicrous. Much too good for her. A long window wrapped right around the side of the building, with a huge vista of the beach and the ocean. This guy was actually *way* more successful than Don Draper. More like...Donald *Trump*. No. Maybe not him. Daisy had always had a thing for older men, but not *that* man. She'd rather date Donald Duck. In fact, dating Donald Duck would actually be really cute. He was so fun and loving. And hey! Her name was Daisy, which was exactly—

"Hello? Anyone there?" asked Montague, motioning for her to take a seat.

"I, uh, I'm not sure I should be...this is too nice." Daisy looked at the light gray brushed suede armchair. Could she really sit on that? She hoped that she didn't somehow look or smell like the trailer she'd stepped out of this morning.

"Resumé," he said, holding out his hand for the paper.

Wow, he really was a man of few words. She handed him the paper, telling herself that at least this would all be over soon. At least she'd be able to hold her head up high for trying.

"Tell me, Daisy Grove," he said, looking at the full name on the paper as he walked round to the big, expensive-looking black leather chair behind his desk. "Why is it that you didn't type up your resumé? Nobody has had the nerve to give me a handwritten resumé in well over two decades. Ever heard of computers?"

"I'm sorry, sir," said Daisy. "My computer broke. And I didn't have time to get to a print shop before this interview."

That was only a small fib. Her computer *had* broken. It's just that it was her ex's computer. And it was at his house. The house she no longer lived in. And she couldn't go to a print shop because after spending a bunch of her money on a fancy milkshake last night–a milkshake she'd never gotten to finish–she couldn't afford it.

"Right," he said, scanning the document. "But you can type, can't you?"

"Oh yes, sir," she said. "I can type sixty words a minute." She could say that with confidence, because it was one-hundred percent true. Her ex-boyfriend had always made her type up the stuff he'd scrawled in his notebooks. Stuff he'd written while drunk at one in the morning. She used to spend hours typing it all up, then he'd just delete it all the next day, saying it was trash.

Montague looked pleased. "That's good." He looked back at the document and his smile faded. "It says here you left school at sixteen. There's no mention of college, or further studies. I take it you have a degree in English, or Journalism, or something similar?"

"Uh, no," said Daisy. "Not exactly, sir. I mean, not at all. I needed money, so I had to work instead of staying in school. But as you can see, I went straight into a copywriting job for a bubble bath company."

"Copywriting for a bubble bath company?" he asked, deadpan. "At sixteen?"

This wasn't a total lie, either. Her friend, Kiera, did run a bubble bath company. It was still– just about – going all these years later. Kiera had let Daisy help her come up with the names of some of the original concoctions. There was Fizz Pop, Whizz Bang, and Sparkle Splash. She still sold products under those names and they'd been a huge success.

"What about after that?" he said, wiping away a big clump of glitter. The glitter fell onto his pants and he swiped it away with an expression of distaste. "It says here you wrote copy for a novelist for six years."

Daisy swallowed. "Yes. I wrote all of the blurbs for the backs of the books." She paused. "And if I'm being honest, I wrote some of the text inside the books, too. They were fiction, but I'm equally at home with non-fiction."

Montague frowned. "You co-wrote the novels?"

"Um, not exactly. They were all published under his name. I mean, I was kind of like his PA, really."

"Wait. You were a copywriter, or a PA?"

Daisy's heart was starting to race. This wasn't going well. Nothing that she was saying now was untrue, it was just all so complicated. Her boyfriend had self-published fantasy novels while they were together, only he'd never gotten the books written in time for the publication deadlines on Amazon, so she'd always ended up finishing them. Plus, she'd had to do the blurbs and make the covers. He didn't pay her a cent for her time, and he insisted that she have a full-time job while they were together, too, so that she could support them.

She'd been stupid to do it for so long, really. Publishing all those books under his name, letting him take the credit. Not that there was much credit to be taken. He wasn't a great writer, and neither was she. The only thing she'd ever been good at was being a submissive woman who'd run around after him doing everything he'd told her to do, no matter what.

"I did a bit of everything," she said. "I wrote the copy. I did the admin. I made the coffees. I mean, I also worked as a barista while I was doing this stuff, because the work for the novelist didn't exactly pay—"

Oh crap. Now she'd really blown it. She *had* worked as a barista, of course, because the bubble bath gig and the cleaning up after her pig of an ex-boyfriend gig weren't exactly lucrative. But admitting to this made her look completely and utterly—

"You know how to make coffee?"

"Yes, I most certainly do," said Daisy, sensing a glimmer of hope. It felt good to be asked something in her comfort zone. Coffee she was great at.

CHAPTER 3 - DAISY

Greater than great.

Montague's expression changed all of a sudden. He went from staring at her as though she was dirt on his shoe to staring at her as though she was some kind of small, fluffy pet. "Tell you what," he said. "Go to the staff room at the end of that corridor, just on the left. You'll find an Expobar Onyx Pro 3 Group Espresso Machine. A stunning piece of machinery. I bought it last week."

Daisy had never heard of such a machine, but she'd worked with a ton of different machines over the years, and they always seemed roughly the same to her.

"Make me a tall, half-caff, soy latte at one-twenty degrees," he said. "And listen up, because this part is very important." He stared at her. "*No* nuts."

Daisy nodded. "Got it. No nuts."

"I have an allergy," Montague said. "Nuts would be very bad for me."

"Understood, sir," said Daisy, giving him a salute for no good reason whatsoever.

Daisy started making her way out of the room, wondering if she should have already taken off her coat. She felt very self-conscious about it after Montague's comment yesterday, but she also felt self-conscious of the fact that she had no clean clothes and nobody else here was dressed like a Little. Why would they be? This was a sober, serious place of work.

"And Daisy?" Montague said.

She turned. "Yes, sir?"

"Go easy on the foam. And bonus points if you make it upside-down."

"Yes, sir," she said quietly. She paused. "Um, is this still part of the interview, sir?"

His eyes bored into her. "Maybe."

There were many things that Daisy Grove was not very good at, but making coffee was not one of them. And luckily, working at a busy Starbucks for several years meant that she was used to getting a zillion different coffee orders every day. In fact, the "upside-down latte" had been part of Starbucks' secret menu for years. A special treat for customers in the know.

She had this in the bag.

She returned with the coffee, beaming with pride as she handed it over. "I did some latte art on top," she said, unable to hide her grin. "It's the company logo. But don't worry, I went easy on the foam. And it's upside-down, of course."

Montague looked genuinely shocked. "Linda had no clue what I was talking about when I asked her to make it upside-down. She spilled coffee all over the floor."

"You just reverse the espresso and milk," Daisy said. "It's easy when you know how. It's basically just a latte macchiato."

Montague blinked at her. "You like your coffee, huh?"

"I do," Daisy said, eyeing the cup enviously. "I like it a ton." She paused. She hoped it didn't seem like she was trying to steal his drink. "But also, I like getting things right for people. That's kind of why I ended up doing a little bit of everything in all my jobs. I'm a people-pleaser, I guess."

Was she saying the right things? Was this going well? At least she hadn't lied in a good while. He was getting to see the real her now.

Montague stared at her for a while longer. His steely eyes gave so little away. Finally, he pushed a button on his phone intercom system. "Linda," he said into the receiver. "You're fired."

Daisy's jaw dropped. Linda was *fired*? The woman who had been so sweet to her while she was waiting to be seen?

Montague looked at Daisy with a smile. "You're hired, young lady," he said. "You'll be my new PA."

"But... I wasn't interviewing for that position," said Daisy.

"You're much better suited to this role," Montague replied. "Frankly, my dear, your copywriting experience is patchy. But with regards to the other position, you are exactly what I'm looking for."

Exactly what I'm looking for.

CHAPTER 3 - DAISY

Nobody had ever said those words to Daisy before.

"You'll be spending a lot of time with me from now on," he said. "And just so you know, you're on probation. Which means you can be fired at a moment's notice. And... I don't like mistakes."

Daisy swallowed. This wasn't her plan. This had never been her plan. But this was going to work out just fine. Right?

CHAPTER 4 - MONTAGUE

"You should be able to sprint five miles in less than thirty minutes, Monty. It's easy. If you can't do it, you're some kind of halfwit, son."

That's what Hubert Manners, Montague's father, used to tell him. He used to make Montague sprint laps around the pool every morning before school. But just because Hubert Manners had won first place in a marathon once, that didn't mean Montague was automatically some kind of superstar athlete. One time, Montague got so dizzy running round and round the pool that he'd fallen into the water. When he came out, he'd been crying.

"Pathetic," Hubert had told him. "Real men don't cry."

And that was the last time that Montague had ever cried. He couldn't be sure if he'd ever laughed after that, either.

That had been almost forty years ago. So much had happened since then. Montague had grown up and started his own business. Hubert had died of a heart attack at sixty-three. And yet, still, Montague couldn't master running five miles in under half an hour.

"What's wrong with me?" he panted on the treadmill.

It was dumb to ask the question, really, because he could list a hundred things. His graying hair. His forehead lines. His constant bad mood.

When he was younger, he'd always felt bullied by his dad. Not to mention he hadn't appreciated his dad's nasty word choices. Not a very politically correct man, and not a very nice one. But ever since he'd died three months ago, Montague had understood something important: His father had wanted the best for him. He'd pushed him because he cared. And even though his father was gone now, Montague still wanted to make him proud.

"Come on, slowpoke!" he yelled at himself, willing his legs to move faster. But it was no use. His body was built in a certain way. He had limitations that he just couldn't transcend.

He turned the speed on the treadmill down slightly so that he was able to keep up without shooting off the end of the damn thing.

He tried to feel better about his inevitable finishing time of thirty-three and a half minutes. That's what it always was when he pushed himself. Thirty-three and a half. Wasn't there a George Harrison album with a name similar to that? Who knew?

Montague didn't have time for anything anymore. He went from work to the treadmill. The treadmill to the work. His Brikk Lux smartwatch was always telling him to reduce his stress levels, to try a breathing exercise, or a bit of yoga. Not a chance. You needed time for that sort of thing. You'd think a watch of all things would have known that.

As Montague ran, he noticed that the cheese plant in the corner of the gym was drooping a bit. Huh. His cleaner, Sonja, was normally on top of that sort of thing. Granted, it had been hot lately, but that was no excuse. He paid her a small fortune to clean his compound, and he expected perfection.

Maybe he should fire her.

He'd already fired Linda today. Maybe he was growing addicted to firing people. Kinda like a purge.

God, he'd been in a pissy mood lately. He needed to try to control it. He couldn't just get rid of everyone in his life, or he'd have nobody left.

The gym wasn't helping much with the pissy mood, unfortunately. Where were all those fucking happy chemicals everyone talked about? They should have been rushing into his brain about now.

He wiped the sweat off his forehead, cursing loudly.

"Screw it," he said as he switched the treadmill off, not even bothering to walk a little, or do any stretches to cool down. "I just need to make more money," he told the cheese plant, getting his sports bottle and pouring the contents of it into the plant pot. "Making money always makes me feel better." He wiped his face and neck with his sports towel, then grabbed his cellphone.

"Daisy," he said, the moment she picked up. "I need you here now."

"Uh...now?" she asked.

"It's urgent," he told her.

"You want me to come into work at eight in the evening?"

"No," he said. "Not work. I want you to meet me at my home. You know Coral Gables?"

"I...of course," said Daisy.

She sounded tired. He hoped she would live up to his expectations. He had her down as the most submissive Little mouse he'd ever met—perfect for adhering to his every whim. That's what he needed from a PA. Linda had always been a bit too bossy. A bit too stuck in her ways.

"Meet me in half an hour," he told her. "I'll text you the address."

"Half an—"

But Montague didn't wait to hear what Daisy had to say. He'd already hung up.

Montague had been ready to tell Daisy off for being late. In fact, he'd been quite looking forward to it. But as she walked into his home with a full thirty seconds to spare, he knew that she really *was* the goody-two-shoes he'd been waiting for.

Linda had been an okay PA, of course, but she'd put her foot down about certain things. She wouldn't work in the evenings, for example. She'd tried to mother him on occasion too, which he didn't like. He was a Daddy, after all. He didn't need a Mommy. He needed a good little subbie, someone obedient and loyal. Someone who knew how to pour a good cup of coffee.

"Wow," Daisy said, looking at the place. "This is unreal. It's like a hotel. But not like any hotel I've ever been in. It's like the kind of hotel celebrities stay in." No doubt realizing that she was gawping and gushing too much, she covered her mouth with her hand, blushing.

He had to admit, he felt a rush of pride seeing her reaction to his home. He barely thought about it anymore—he supposed he took it all for granted. The marble floors. The spectacular vistas. The Scavolini kitchen and Gaggenau appliances. The six-car garage, and the stylish cabana. He'd worked hard to get it all just how he liked it, but he hadn't had anyone to share it with in a long time. That kinda made him forget what it was like, because he was only ever seeing it through his own jaded eyes.

"Glad you found the place okay," he said. "It's kind of a gated community within a gated community."

"Yeah, no kidding," Daisy said, grinning. "Tahiti Beach is like Fort Knox. You need to have a personal invite from a resident to get into both sets of gates. I'm pretty sure they were looking at me like: 'who's this loser?'"

That was interesting. Daisy didn't seem to think much of herself. She'd taken a big, brave step coming to his office in the first place, then. He hoped that while she worked for him he'd be able to help with her confidence. Although maybe that was wishful thinking on his part. He didn't exactly seem to have a calming effect on people. His grumpy side always got the better of him.

"So, what are we working on tonight, boss?" asked Daisy, looking up at him with her hands on her hips.

Damn, she was a beautiful woman. He was trying his best not to think about her that way. He'd just employed the girl, for godsakes, but seriously. Those big blue eyes, and pouting lips. Those cute yellow glasses, and that submissive streak. She was more than just his perfect PA. She was his perfect type, period.

Stop thinking with your dick, Montague. Work is all that matters. Always has been, always will be.

"Come through to my home office," Montague said. "Oh, and leave your coat on the stand. Don't want to look at that thing for another minute."

Daisy stalled, but then took off her coat shyly. She was wearing something different than she had been earlier. Something faintly ridiculous, actually. It looked like a pajama top with a cartoon Cinderella on it.

"Shoot," she said. "I'm sorry. I figured you were more interested in me making it here on time than making it here wearing proper work clothes. I meant to stuff something in my bag, but I was kinda in a rush…"

CHAPTER 4 - MONTAGUE

Montague saw that she was wearing pajama pants too. Yikes. This was embarrassing for them both. He'd have lent her something, but that would have probably made her feel even worse. Besides, he was touched that she'd prioritized his deadline over anything else. It showed promise.

"You were right to come straight here," he said. "And your interest in cartoon movies may actually help with the job we have to do tonight."

"Are we watching a movie?" Daisy asked hopefully.

"Not a chance," said Montague, leading her to his office.

"Awww, that's a shame." When she reached the office, she stopped. "Okay, I thought the *work* office was good, but this is...wow."

Montague's home office was actually bigger than his work one. It had a gabled ceiling, making the room feel hugely light and airy. The windows went all the way up to the top, and they looked right out onto the beach. Not from a distance, like at work. This was the real deal—they were *on* the beach. Enormous glass doors led straight out onto golden sand, the flat blue ocean just a few yards away from them.

"I spend a lot of time working when I'm at home," Montague said. "So I may as well make my office the best room in the house."

"Most people would use this as a living room, or bedroom," Daisy said. "But it's nice to work in here too. More than nice. I mean, every room in this house is probably amazing, so I'm not trying to disparage—"

"You talk a lot. We'll have to work on that." He motioned for her to take a seat on the couch opposite him. That was one little treat he allowed himself. He didn't always have to sit behind his desk when he worked from home. Sometimes, in the evenings, he let himself sit by the windows, looking out at the water.

Daisy sat and bowed her head, clearly not wanting to be naughty by saying anymore.

He noted that with pleasure. "There's a problem at work," Montague began.

Daisy raised her eyebrows. "Is it something I can—"

Montague raised his hand. "It's nothing to do with the business side of things. That's all going great. It's more of a...staff issue. The staff have been a little...off lately. And I believe it's because the buzz is wearing off."

"The buzz?"

"Making money. We're making a ton, believe me. But I think people want to make more. They want to see the graph going off the charts. They want to see growth so exponential that there isn't even a graph to show the data anymore. They want to see a vertical line going all the way up to the heavens."

Daisy looked confused.

"Disney World," said Montague, jumping up from the couch.

Daisy immediately sat up straight, as though she'd been jolted with electricity.

"It's one of the biggest money-making empires in the world," said Montague. "And I want a piece of that pie."

"You want to own shares in Disney World?" Daisy inquired.

"Nope," said Montague. "I want my own Disney World. I want to create a theme park especially for Littles."

"For Littles, sir?" asked Daisy shyly.

Montague paused. "Didn't anyone at the office fill you in?" He rolled his eyes. "You know about the company, right? You know what Daddies Inc. does?"

Daisy shook her head. "Not exactly, sir...I mean, not at all."

Montague began to pace the room. "Daddies Inc. is a multi-billion-dollar corporation dedicated to giving Bigs and Littles everything they need for their lifestyle. Think: clubs for private members, upscale parties, secret hotel suites, upscale care packages. You name it, we do it. In a way that screams class and luxury, obviously."

"Obviously," she echoed.

She looked—what was that expression? Doleful? Baffled?

He stopped pacing and looked at her. "You do know what a Little is, right? It's just...you seemed a bit awkward when I raised it the other day."

"I, uh...I *do* know what a Little is," Daisy replied.

Montague raised an eyebrow. It was a trick he'd taught himself to do when he was eleven, and it had proven itself to be one of the best things he'd ever learned in life. There were so many times when it seemed fitting to raise an eyebrow, and right now was one of those times. "And you're definitely *not* a Little?"

Daisy shook her head. "Nuh-uh. Not me. No, siree."

"I hope not," he said, his voice turning grave "Or you'd be doubling down on a lie, young lady."

Daisy bit her lip. "So...about this theme park."

"Yes. Indeed," said Montague, pleased to be getting back to work. "Here. Take a notepad and pen. I want you to write down everything I say."

Daisy nodded. "Yes, sir." She looked pleased to be getting on with work, too. Did he make her uncomfortable? He hoped not.

"Feel free to pitch in if you have any ideas, by the way," said Montague. "Theme parks aren't exactly my forte. I bet a girl like you knows a great deal more about them than I do."

Daisy grinned. "Well, I've never been to Disney World, but that's one of the reasons I was attracted to Florida. I'm hoping to save up enough to go there and—"

Just then, Montague's phone made an irritating screeching sound. The sound of nails being dragged down a blackboard. Damn it. That was the ringtone he'd programmed for Olga.

"Sorry," he said. "I'm gonna have to take this."

There were only four people in the world who Montague would have had to take a phone call from at this moment: Bastian, Isaac, Olga, and the President. Not that the President would have any reason to call his phone, but still...if the President calls, you answer.

He strode out the room and shut the door so Daisy couldn't hear him.

"What is it, Olga?" he hissed into the receiver. "Are you calling to say you've finally come to your senses?"

Olga laughed. "Not a chance, dickwad. My lawyer agrees with me. I'm not going to sign the divorce paperwork until you agree to give me the compound."

Montague looked at the four walls around him. The four beautiful walls that he'd built from scratch. Sure, he'd had help from an architect, a bunch of builders, and interior decorators, and all the rest, but it was still his project. His baby. And Olga didn't deserve a damn piece of it. "I'll agree to that when hell freezes over," he told her. "Which might happen quite quickly once *you* get there."

"Are you threatening me?" asked Olga.

He used to like her Russian accent. Now, he wanted to hear it about as much as he wanted nuclear war. "You know, marriage is a contract, Monty. You don't get out of a contract without paying the price."

"You don't deserve a cent," snarled Montague. "You're damn lucky I'm letting you have the houseboat. That thing is basically a floating mansion."

"You know I get seasick."

"Not my problem!" Montague spat, hanging up on her.

Shit.

His heart rate was spiking and if he hadn't had company, he'd have yelled an expletive or two, and maybe hurled something very hard at something else.

But he couldn't do that, so he put on his best neutral expression and went back into the office.

"Are you okay, sir?" Daisy asked, standing up. "I heard shouting. And you're looking kinda beetroot colored. Are you well?"

"I'm fine," said Montague. "Just a little worked up. Not a phone call I should have taken, it turns out."

Daisy chewed on her pen. "Maybe we should take a breather for five minutes? Do something fun? That always helps me calm down when I get worked up."

Montague felt a surge of irritation. "Five minutes of fun? Out of the question. We need to work."

He felt a pulsing vibration on his wrist. He knew that sensation. It was his Brikk smartwatch telling him to relax. Telling him that if he wasn't careful, he'd end up going the same way as his old man.

"Fine," he said. "Five minutes. But I'm setting a timer." He pushed a couple buttons on his watch and looked at the timer, satisfied that the five minutes was already reducing. Four minutes fifty-nine. Four minutes fifty-eight. He turned to Daisy. "So, what do you suggest?"

CHAPTER 5 - DAISY

There were some things you could never say to your boss. And there were some things that you could never, *ever* say to your boss in his own home. Here were some of those things.

Let's slide around on all the polished marble floors!
Hey, are you up for a water fight in your amazing pool?
How about we strip off our clothes and race to the ocean?

Daisy couldn't help feeling like this was some kind of test. She was still on her probationary period as a PA. What if she suggested something so dumb he fired her just as easily as he'd fired his last PA?

She looked out of the windows at the beach, wondering if suggesting building sandcastles would sound too silly and childish. She kept swearing that she wasn't a Little, after all. Grown-up women didn't build sandcastles. Besides, it seemed very unlikely that a man like Montague would have a bucket and spade handy.

She racked her brains. It was embarrassing enough that she had turned up in her pajamas tonight. The truth of the matter was that she had been so tired lately that she had been asleep when Montague called. Still groggy, she hadn't realized what she was wearing until she was halfway to Coral Gables, by which time it was too late. Montague hadn't commented on them, but then, he didn't seem that interested in other people.

"Let's see..." she said, tapping her hand against her chin. "What kind of stuff makes you smile?"

Montague looked at her with the most un-smiley expression she'd ever seen.

"Oh. Okay. Um. Well, if you're not really the smiling sort, then..."

Montague perhaps sensed her discomfort, because he surprised her by stepping in. "I have an idea," he said. "Follow me."

Daisy followed him out of the room and along the corridor, past about a zillion closed doors, until they eventually stopped.

"This is my games room," he told her.

Daisy grew excited. A games room? She couldn't believe that serious Montague had something as frivolous as a games room! What would be in there? A giant Connect Four? A trampoline? Laser tag?

"Here we go," said Montague, pushing open the door. "My golf simulator."

Daisy took in the enormous LCD screen across the back wall and the rectangle of neat green carpet in front of it. She tried to resist the urge to snicker. A golf simulator. Of all the ways to kick back and relax, playing pretend golf was not one of them in her book.

"What's up?" asked Montague, switching on the screen. "You don't know how to play?"

"Not...exactly."

"Well, have you ever played miniature golf?"

"You mean teeny tiny golf balls and golf clubs the size of matchsticks?" asked Daisy. She was being a little impish, but at least she was enjoying herself.

Montague ignored her, flicking through a number of settings on the golf game. He changed the difficulty rating to *easy*, and then he selected *kid mode*. "This isn't the type of course I'd normally play on the Full Swing Golf Simulator. You know, Tiger Woods has this exact same setup in his home."

"Tiger Woods? Oh, wow," Daisy said, pretending to know what Montague was talking about. Tiger Woods was a funny name. A bit like...Lion Forest. Or...Cheetah Grove. No, wait. Grove was *her* surname. She snickered.

"Tiger probably doesn't play this course, though." Montague picked a course called "Windmill Madness" and suddenly, the course that appeared before them looked exactly like the kind of place Daisy wanted to play in. The grass was pink, the windmills had cartoon faces, and for some reason, there were mischievous-looking mice running around, stopping every now and then to squeak in time to the upbeat tempo music.

44

CHAPTER 5 - DAISY

"Here's your club, madam," said Montague, affecting a British accent.

"Oh, thank you, kind sir." Daisy giggled.

Montague showed her how to lift her club back in the air to take a swing, and Daisy stuck out her butt and gave it a little wiggle because she *swore* she'd seen professionals do that on TV.

"Watch out, or I'll spank that thing," Montague teased, and he immediately stiffened up, uncomfortable, as though he'd made a faux-pas.

Daisy wasn't sure how to let him know that she didn't mind a bit. They were having fun right now, being silly. She knew he didn't mean it. Here she was, standing in his uber-expensive luxury home wearing Cinderella pajamas and wiggling her butt around like a big kid. Of *course* he didn't want to spank her ass.

Plus, it's not like he was a Daddy Dom. There wasn't an ounce of protectiveness in his soul. He might have been a straight Dom, but she even doubted that. Doms were just playing a role, they weren't cruel for the sake of it. They were acting out their sub's fantasies. It was hard to imagine Montague taking the time to act out anyone's fantasies other than his own.

Trying to direct her attention back to the game, she swung her golf club like Montague showed her, but her ball flew up into the sky, hit an inexplicably flying mouse, bounced off a windmill propeller, and landed in a puddle of purple goo.

"Darn!" she shouted. "So close, but no cigar!"

Montague shook his head, tutting. Would this be the first time she'd see him smile? "Here's how it's done, Little one," he said, swinging back his club.

Just then, an alarm went off. Montague *hadn't* smiled, as it happened, and now he was frowning.

"Ah well," he said. "Five minutes are up."

Daisy looked up at him. "Aren't you at least going to finish your turn?" She really, really didn't want to stop playing this game. She *had* to know whether she could ever get out of that purple goo.

"Sorry, little mouse," he said. "Time is money."

Disappointed as she was, she couldn't help noting with some satisfaction that he'd given her a nickname. It felt good. Like he was loosening up a little around her.

But when they went back to his office, he was anything but loose. With a grimly set jaw, he talked through his ideas for the theme park. What amazed Daisy was that he used a bunch of facts and figures, but he didn't once talk about the rides.

As she struggled to keep up with his stream of words, she rubbed her eyes and could barely stifle a yawn.

"Need a coffee?" Montague asked her. "I've got another couple hours to get through yet."

Daisy glanced nervously at the clock. "Sir, it's gone eleven-thirty. I'm not sure I can stay awake much longer." She yawned again. "Is it normal to work this late?"

"It's entirely normal," Montague snapped. "You know, maybe you're not the right person for this job."

"No, no, I am," said Daisy. "I just...haven't been getting too much sleep lately. One of my neighbors, he...never mind. Uh, yeah, sure. I'll take that coffee, please."

"It's the same machine as the one at work," Montague said. "Kitchen's second on the left. I take mine black at this hour."

Oh. So he wasn't offering to make coffee for her. Well. Made sense. He was the boss, after all.

"Black," echoed Daisy, with another yawn. "No problemo."

Montague, who up until now had not stopped pacing the room, stopped and looked down at her.

Daisy wasn't sure what it was that swayed him. Maybe it was the rings under her eyes. The frizzy, mussed-up hair. The constant yawning. Or maybe it was the fact she was wearing her gosh-darn pajamas. Whatever it was, he seemed to take pity on her.

"You know what?" he said. "We can pick this up in the morning. I don't seem to have the same body clock as everyone else. Different circadian rhythm. I can survive on four hours sleep because it's so well-balanced. Ninety minutes deep sleep. Ninety minutes REM. The rest light sleep. I've trained myself over the years." He pointed at his smartwatch. "This thing rates me at least a ninety for my sleep every night without fail."

Daisy looked at the gold watch her boss was showing her, studded with diamonds, like stars in the night sky. Somehow, the sight of those diamonds made her even sleepier. "I need to call a cab."

"Nonsense," Montague replied. "My driver will take you back."

Daisy considered it, but knew that much as she wanted to, she couldn't accept. There was no way that Montague could find out where she lived. It was much too embarrassing. Especially now that she'd seen *his* home.

"I'd prefer to take a cab," Daisy said sleepily. "Just one of my weird quirks."

"Fine. Then let me call it for you," said Montague. "Where are you headed?"

This wasn't going well. It felt impossible to keep the truth from him where rides home were concerned.

"Actually, I think I'll just walk," she said. She was too tired to think of a better plan. She'd just keep walking until she had gone past both sets of gates, and then she'd hail down a cab. Or maybe she'd just walk all the way back. She didn't really have the money for a cab. It would be...easy...peasy.

"Daisy? You're talking with your eyes closed. You all right, little mouse?"

"I'm a little mouse," she said, sticking her thumb in her mouth. "Squeak." She yawned, rubbed her eyes, then lay down and fell fast asleep on her boss's luxurious and extremely comfortable couch.

CHAPTER 6 - MONTAGUE

How had he only managed a rating of eighty-one percent for his sleep last night?

Montague looked at his smartwatch grumpily, wondering if it was time he bought a new one. Eighty-one percent. Might as well have been a big fat zero. No point having even gone to bed for that. Pah.

He could practically hear his father's voice rattling around in his head.

"Not good enough, Monty, you dumb animal."

Monty trudged back upstairs from the kitchen, trying to put a lid on his self-loathing. If it hadn't been for the issue with his sleep, he'd have been in a rather good mood, actually. The thing was, having Daisy in his house had actually felt quite...nice. That was part of the reason he hadn't slept so well last night. He'd found himself thinking about her instead of sleeping. Wondering what she thought of him, wondering what she was dreaming about. Wondering, wondering, wondering.

This morning, he'd woken up a little early too, wanting to get a few things ready before she woke. Last night, he'd instantly regretted asking her to make them both a coffee when they were at his house. She was his guest, in his home. *He* should have been the one to refresh her. So, this morning, he'd done his best to make amends.

He knocked softly on the bedroom door and forced himself to wait a few moments before knocking again.

"Don't be impatient, son," he imagined his father saying to him. *"It's a nasty habit of yours. Along with all the other stuff. Biting your nails. Excessive masturbation. Being a Daddy Dom. Disgusting, Monty."*

"Shut up, father," he whispered to himself. "You don't know anything about me. You're dead. This is all just a figment of my imagination."

"Hello?" called a sweet, little voice from inside the room.

He opened the door a crack. "All right if I come in?"

"Yes, Daddy, of course!" Daisy said, clearly not even realizing the mistake she'd just made.

He went into the room and was pleased to see how at home she looked in there. Last night he'd carried her up to bed, removed her glasses, and tucked her in. He suspected that this room was the most fitting for her, and now that she was awake in it, he could see that he'd gotten it right.

"This room is amazing," she gushed. "I can't believe you have something like this in your house. A bed shaped like a royal carriage! Fireworks painted on the wall! It's like waking up in a fairy-tale!" She paused. "But...I don't remember coming up to bed..."

"I carried you," Montague informed her stiffly. "I hope you don't mind. I thought you'd be more comfortable here. Nothing strange—"

"It's okay," Daisy said. "I appreciate it. That was the best night's sleep I've had in weeks. I feel like a..."

"New woman?" hazarded Montague.

"Princess!" Daisy answered with a giggle.

He looked at her blond hair, bleached so light that it was almost white. It looked dry as straw, sticking up almost vertically, and he thought what a funny princess she'd make. It seemed strange to see her without her glasses on, too. She looked adorable with her spectacles, but now, like this, with those big blue eyes, she looked...dangerous.

"Take a shower," Montague said, motioning to the door at the other end of the room. All the bedrooms in this place had ensuite bathrooms, of course. "Then I'll meet you downstairs for breakfast."

"Breakfast? You really don't need to..." Daisy's tummy made a loud gurgle at that moment, and she blushed. "Well, all right then. Maybe just something light. But don't go to too much trouble."

Montague left her room and went downstairs, pouring her freshly-brewed coffee into a travel mug, and wrapping her toast in aluminum foil. When she came downstairs, she looked bright-eyed and bushy-tailed. If it wasn't for her slightly grubby-looking *Cinderella* pajamas, she'd have looked raring to go.

"What's for breakfast?" she asked, looking around at the empty dining table and clear kitchen surfaces.

"I made you toast," said Montague. "Wasn't sure how you liked it, so went for butter and jelly with the crusts cut off. It's usually a crowd-pleaser."

"You cut the crusts off?" Daisy gasped. "I had no idea you were such a gentleman, Mr. Manners."

He liked it when she teased him a little. As long as she didn't get sassy. If she got too impertinent, he'd have to fight the very strong, very inappropriate urge to redden that peachy ass of hers. An ass which, obviously, he hadn't checked out once, since that also would have been very inappropriate.

"I made coffee too," said Montague. "Assumed you'd like it milky in the morning."

"Wow, this is too good to be true," Daisy said, grinning from ear-to-ear.

Montague handed her the travel mug and foil-wrapped toast. "We're going to eat it *en route*."

"Ah, there's the old boss," she said playfully. Then, slightly panicked, she paused. "I thought we didn't start work for another hour?"

"We don't," he replied. "I'm taking you shopping first."

"Shopping? At eight in the morning?"

"There's a boutique I know that'll be open already," he told her as they vacated the house and headed for the garage. "Can't have you walking around in your pajamas all day. I'm going to get you some work clothes. It's the least I can do after making you work so late that you fell asleep on my couch."

It had been such a long time since he'd had the opportunity to care for anyone like this and he felt rusty. He hoped he was getting it right.

Daisy seemed taken aback. "That's...so kind of you. But really—"

"Don't even think about refusing," he said. "I insist." He looked at the poor thing, wearing that ugly brown monstrosity over her shabby pajamas. "Besides, I'm getting you a new damn coat while we're at it."

As she climbed into the car, she appeared speechless. He hoped that it was good speechless, and not offended speechless. Maybe it was a bit of both.

"By the way," he said. "Try not to get crumbs in the Bentley, eh?"

Daisy looked at him and shook her head.

But he could see that there was a flicker of enjoyment in her eyes. He was sure of it. Hundred percent.

Montague had never enjoyed shopping with a woman before. With Daisy, though, it was a lot of fun.

After a little coaxing and reassurance that money really was no object—and she could have as many outfits as she wanted—she had agreed to go with it. In fact, she had tried on the most outrageous stuff in the shop, laughing her head off at how funny she had looked in some of the more sophisticated numbers, and how uncomfortable some of the sexy black dresses were.

Finally, with advice from the store owner, she had picked out a bunch of clothes from the *Inner Child* range. That was the whole reason Montague had brought her to this store. There was a special back room of clothes that only certain customers got to see. Montague hadn't wanted to push Daisy into anything, and she kept swearing that she wasn't a Little, despite every sign in the universe pointing in the opposite direction. However, Montague had a hunch that she'd love the clothes, and he was right.

She'd chosen a floral dress, a pink flare dress with green frogs all over it, some mint-green overalls, a red pinafore, yellow striped leggings, and a variety of cute sweaters that went perfectly with her glasses. He'd been delighted when she'd popped out of the changing rooms to show him a few of the combinations that she had on, and he had to admit, she looked sexier in those *Inner Child* outfits than any of the little black dresses she'd tried on earlier.

Once she was done and wearing a new outfit of her choice, he'd picked out a coat for her. A yellow rain mac, with a belt at the waist and a hood to keep her dry. He was confident that she'd love it, as the color matched her glasses, and thankfully, he'd been right about that, too.

Even so, she looked hesitant. "I, er, normally go for something a little more...austere on the outside."

Montague was puzzled. "Everything else about you is so bright, so fun. Why do you feel the need to hide that?"

Daisy bit her lip. "Not everyone appreciates my sunny side."

He wondered if this was a code. Was he talking about the fact that she was embarrassed about being a Little? He didn't want to probe too deeply in case he touched a nerve.

"Come on," he said. "Let's go. We have time to grab another coffee on the way into work if we're quick."

Daisy whooped, running out the store like she had no cares in the world.

He liked seeing her like this. Hoped that he'd see her like this again.

"I'll never be able to repay you for all the stuff you just bought me," said Daisy. "You'll have to take it out of my paychecks for, like, the rest of time."

"Seriously, it was nothing," said Montague. "In fact, I like supporting that store. It's part of the Daddies Inc. family, after all."

She eyed him suspiciously. "It is?"

"Sure," he said. "We have encouraged a number of high-end stores around the States to run labels for women who prefer more...youthful attire."

Daisy blushed. She seemed too bashful to question him further.

They headed for the coffee shop, laughing at a cloud in the sky that Daisy noticed looked like an elephant.

Hold on to this, Montague, he told himself. *This freewheeling sense of fun and joy. This woman who's teaching you how to live again.*

But the moment they arrived at work, the big fat raincloud reappeared over Montague's head. The staff looked glummer than ever, and he got the distinct feeling they were whispering about him as he walked past. Worse than that, they seemed to be whispering about Daisy too.

"They're all staring at me," Daisy said quietly. "I knew this coat was too much."

"If they are, they're just jealous," he said. "It's a very good coat."

"It is," she replied. He could tell that she was trying to appear cheerful, but it was hard. People were looking at her, shaking their heads.

Well, screw them. He'd fire them all if he had to.

They had a meeting first thing, so they headed to the boardroom and Daisy took off her coat and hung it on the back of her chair. She looked like a knockout in her new outfit, and she looked a little more confident now that they were among the higher echelons of staff. Bastion, Isaac, and Sam. There was no way that any of these guys were going to be cruel to the girl. These guys were basically pussycats.

"Well, asshole?" began Bastion, his arms folded and his eyes boring into him. "You got any great ideas? I haven't got all fucking day."

Daisy shifted in her seat, shocked. Her pretty floral dress made a pleasing ruffle sound as she fidgeted.

Shit, man. Concentrate.

"Uh... hang on a sec," said Montague. "I haven't introduced you to Daisy yet. She's my new PA."

No one in the room seemed to be able to look at her. What was their problem?

Isaac coughed. "Er, what did you fire Linda for?"

He was shocked at the abrupt change in subject, but he answered with indignation. "She nearly killed me."

Isaac looked aghast. "She did?"

"It was a nut thing," Montague replied.

Isaac's expression of shock turned into one of confusion. He turned to Daisy. "It's good to meet you, Miss. We're just a bit surprised that Montague fired the company PA without talking to any of us about it first. She's been a loyal member of staff for—"

"Didn't anyone hear me?" Montague snapped. He could feel his blood pressure rising again. All the good that being with Daisy had done him outside of work was being undone in mere minutes. "I *said* the woman almost killed me!"

"Next time, I'd really appreciate it if you brought it to my attention first," Sam said. "She requires a month's notice period, and a severance package based on her years of service—"

"Not if she tries to kill me," Montague butted in.

"You two can hash that out later," boomed Bastion, clearly sick of the conversation. "Right now, I want to know what your plan is to save this company."

Montague stole a sideways glance at Daisy, who looked concerned. Well, damn, this was an embarrassing way to start their working relationship together.

"The company is doing great," said Montague defensively. "It's just the small matter of staff morale."

"Made much worse by the constant hirings and firings," said Sam moodily, although at least he cast Daisy an apologetic look after saying it.

"Lucky for you," said Montague, "Daisy and I worked late last night."

"We're not interested in your sex life," Bastion informed him, rolling his eyes.

"Whatever you're insinuating, you're on the wrong track," said Montague. "Daisy has the makings of the best PA this company has ever seen."

"She'll only be the second PA this company has ever seen," said Isaac, splitting hairs as usual.

"And Linda was very good—" began Sam.

Montague raised a finger, indicating that everyone needed to be quiet. He walked to the front of the room, plugged his laptop into the screen, and fired up Keynote.

"Last night," he said, "Daisy and I worked on a presentation."

Daisy looked up at him with an expression of panic on her face.

He tried to shoot her back a look that let her know she didn't need to worry. He had stayed up an extra couple hours after she'd fallen asleep on his couch and using her excellent notes he'd knocked this together quickly and efficiently.

He pressed the first button on his Keynote slideshow and admired the picture of Mickey Mouse that came on his screen. "It's Disney World," he said proudly. "For Bigs and Littles."

Everyone in the boardroom looked confused.

"You want to build a theme park for Littles?" Bastion asked at last.

"Indeed I do," said Montague. "Let me talk you through the fact and figures. The moneymaking potential is off the charts. It's sure to bring the buzz back to you all."

Halfway through the presentation, Bastion stood up. "This is a very interesting business proposition," he said, pausing to take a long sip of water. "But it doesn't help one fucking bit."

"What do you mean?" Montague asked, trying not to sound hurt.

"It's just...work, sir," Sam explained. "It's just more work. I'm not sure that the staff morale will be increased with...more work."

Montague knitted his brow together. He was more than confused. "But... more work means more money. And more money means more morale. Everyone knows that, right?"

"No," said Sam, shaking his head. "That's not right I'm afraid, Mr. Manners. The staff here are all very happy with their pay."

"I'm sure they'd be happier with a fat bonus check around Christmas time when this thing starts to pay off—"

"No," Sam said again. "There are some things money can't buy, Montague. Surely you can see that."

Montague thought about this in relation to his own life. He couldn't think of anything that money hadn't been able to buy him throughout his life. Cars, houses, pools, golf simulators. Hell, it even bought him a marriage at one point...but then again, look at how that worked out.

Just then, Daisy cleared her throat. "I haven't been here very long," she said. "But I guess I'm a fresh pair of eyes? I have a few ideas about how we could increase staff morale around here."

Everyone turned to look at her.

Montague wished there was some signal he could give to shut her up. The girl had good intentions, but she was just a PA on day one of working for a company she understood almost nothing about. If she said something out of line in front of all the most senior members of the company, she'd be out on her ear quicker than you could say "safeword."

CHAPTER 6 - MONTAGUE

"Maybe you'll think my ideas are silly," she said, "but I noticed yesterday when I was waiting for my interview that not everyone likes the taste of the water in the water cooler."

"It's enriched with important minerals," said Montague. "They increase productivity."

"Let the girl speak," Bastion interjected.

"Well...maybe as an alternative we could set up a, like, juice station in the corner."

"A juice station?" Montague repeated incredulously.

"Yeah, making smoothies and juices is fun," said Daisy enthusiastically. "And healthy, too. And maybe on hot days, we could have a slushy machine too. Just because, well, because everyone likes slushies."

"Everyone likes slushies," Montague repeated in a monotone voice that suggested he could hardly believe he was hearing this. Hell, if someone else wasn't about to fire her ass right now, then maybe he was.

"Do all your ideas involve beverages?" Bastion asked, leaning forward on his elbows, scrutinizing her.

"No," she said. "I've noticed that people are expected to work long hours around here. Maybe there could be a nap corner?"

Montague was tempted to pinch himself. "A. Nap. Corner."

"They have one at Google," said Isaac, a stickler for pointing out the goddamn facts once again.

"And maybe a games room," said Daisy, casing a shy glance at Montague. "Doesn't have to be golf, but, like, you know, cheap stuff like table tennis. And possibly a place for people to just relax on beanbags and read a while. Or people could read aloud to each other."

"Juice. Naps. Games. Reading aloud," Bastion boomed. "What you're saying is... that our office should be run like a theme park for Littles?"

"No. Yes. I don't know. Sorry, sir," said Daisy, flustered. She looked over at Montague. "I guess maybe I was getting my idea confused with your idea."

Sam stood up, his chair screeching on the floor. "You know what? You're on to something. We have been so focused on our customers that we've

57

forgotten about what's happening at home. Some of our staff members are Littles. *You're* clearly a Little too, Daisy."

Daisy's cheeks turned bright red. "No. I'm not."

"We should think about this," Bastion enthused. "If it's good enough for Google—"

"The staff at Google are kind of anarchic," said Isaac. "Apparently, their productivity levels aren't fantastic these days—"

"But *their* staff members aren't necessarily Littles. And they don't have a bunch of Daddies in charge of the company, keeping them in check."

Montague never blushed, but if he had been a blushing man, he would have blushed about now. He hadn't told Daisy that he was a Daddy Dom yet, and for some reason, he felt awkward about it being revealed to her like this.

"We have to go now, Daisy," Montague said, unplugging his laptop and starting to leave the room. "We'll talk more about these ideas later. Daisy will type them up and email them to you all over the weekend."

Daisy followed him out of the room. "I'm really sorry, sir," she said awkwardly. "I wasn't trying to upstage you. And now I understand why working last night was so important. There's a crisis with staff morale. If I'd realized what was at stake, I'd have tried to stay up to help you with the presentation."

Montague marched ahead a few paces, then turned, full of anger. "Why didn't you tell me you're a Little, Daisy?"

"I... I..."

"I first ran into you in a bar for Littles. You came to my house in *Cinderella* pajamas. You love juice, and naps, and games."

"That doesn't necessarily mean that I'm—"

"You laugh like nothing else matters. You twirl your hair when you're feeling shy. You suck your thumb in your sleep. You wear clothes that make you look ten years younger. You're a Little, Daisy. I know it."

Daisy looked taken aback. "You really noticed all that stuff about me? In less than twenty-four hours?"

Montague nodded. "The only thing I *don't* like about you being a Little,"

CHAPTER 6 - MONTAGUE

Montague continued, "is that you keep lying to me about it. When we first met, I asked if you were a Little because I was *hoping* you'd say yes. I like working with Littles. My last PA, Linda, wasn't a Little. She was more of a… caregiver. Not as submissive as I'd have liked. But you. *You.*"

Daisy bit her lip. "Are you…a Daddy?"

Montague felt that would-be beetroot flush again, knowing that his skin was in fact staying just the same color as always. Inside, though, he felt like he was pure adrenaline. "Listen," he said. "Those ideas you had…Maybe they'll work, maybe they won't. But I'd like to talk to you more. It's Saturday tomorrow. How about we get dinner?"

She looked despondent. "Oh. Yes. A work meeting on a Saturday," she said flatly. "And then I'll type up that staff email. I love working weekends."

"It's not a work meeting," Montague said, looking deep into Daisy's eyes.

Daisy wrung her hands. "Wh-what is it then?"

His gaze flicked down at her mouth for a moment, then back up again. "It's an experiment."

CHAPTER 7 - DAISY

———

"Okay, we're calling it. This is another intervention." Kiera lined up about twenty different bottles of bubble bath on the rickety table in Daisy's trailer. "First thing's first, you're having a long bubble bath."

Daisy shook her head. "Kiera, I don't *have* a bath in my trailer. I don't even have a shower."

Kiera looked revolted. "Please tell me you have a toilet."

"I have a toilet."

Kiera wrinkled her nose. "But where do you wash?"

"There's a communal shower over the other side of the park. But I don't really use it much because it's…"

Disgusting?

Terrifying?

Mostly broken?

"…not that convenient," Daisy found herself saying.

Peach, who had been trying, one-handed, to sort drinks for them all while holding her little white Shih Tzu, Teddy, in her other hand, turned around. "Not that convenient? You kidding me, Daisy? This place is a dive. It's worse than a dive. It's a literal hellhole."

Daisy knew she was right, but she pouted anyway. "You're talking about my *home*."

"Daisy, you've been hiding out here for two weeks. This is *not* your home. Your home is in Connecticut with us."

"Technically, I don't have an address there since I left Raymond."

"I don't want to hear that name ever again," Kiera announced moodily as she packed her bubble baths back in her bag.

"If you don't want me to talk about the fiancé I walked out on," Daisy

61

huffed, "then why are you guys here?"

Peach brought three cracked glasses of cloudy water over to the table and then sat down with Teddy on her lap.

Teddy was wearing a new blue bow to tie back the topknot in his hair and he gave Daisy a supercute look. A look that said: *We's all missin' you, Daisy!* She tried to ignore his supercuteness and the supercute voice she'd just given him in her head.

"And by the way," Daisy continued grumpily, "how did you find me? I haven't told anyone I'm here."

Peach leaned forward, taking Daisy's hand. "Daisy. Where's our sunshine girl gone? I could just...*throw* things at that good-for-nothing ex of yours."

"You've still got your Find My Friends app running," Kiera explained. "That's how we found you."

"Ah." Daisy had installed that app on her phone three years ago, back when things with Raymond started to get bad. Well, they had always been bad, but at that point, they had started to get even worse. Raymond liked to keep tabs on her, tracking her every move. Not trusting Raymond, Daisy had shared the app with her friends too, as a way of having *them* keep tabs on him. At least if she went missing or something, they might be able to rescue her.

Luckily, that had never happened. Raymond had never tried to kidnap her or anything like that. It was all psychological. *Gaslighting* was probably the best way to describe it. It was only in recent months that Daisy had been able to recognize it for what it truly was. Discounting her achievements. Minimizing her feelings. Calling her overly sensitive when she got upset. Making her question her own version of reality.

He was jealous and possessive, too. Not in a sexy, protective, man-bear kind of a way. In a way that involved checking up on her every five minutes. Not letting her hang out with any male friends.

It was a suffocating relationship. From the outside, it was probably impossible for anyone to understand why she'd stayed with Raymond so long. *Six years.* Daisy guessed that it was partly because she'd wanted so badly for everything to be okay that she'd convinced herself it was. And it was partly because she'd been scared.

She was determined not to be scared anymore, though. And part of that involved learning to be independent. Discovering who she really was.

"Look, you guys," said Daisy, "I really appreciate you both coming here. I know how much you care about me, and I care about you both, too. But you two have your lives figured out. Kiera, you run your own business. Peach, you have your work at the pet rescue center."

Peach shook her head. "Daisy, we have problems, just like you. But we're stronger together. You know that." She put on a cutesy voice as she wiggled Teddy's paws around. "My highly-trained paws are at your service!"

Daisy couldn't help giggling. Peach was a *PAW Patrol* nut. She was always quoting the catchphrases from the show. So much so, that although Daisy had never watched a single episode of the show, she still knew a ton about it. The names of the characters, some of their basic traits, their slogans. It was infectious.

"I hate to say it, Daze," Kiera began, "but if it hadn't been for us, you'd probably be married to that lunatic right now and on your honeymoon in Paris."

Daisy sighed, remembering everything that happened two weeks ago. "It was just...a lot. You guys staging an actual intervention on the morning of my wedding day. I felt so...small."

"You needed to hear the truth."

"Maybe I needed to make my own mistakes," Daisy countered. She didn't want to blame her friends for what had happened, but it was hard not to feel like she needed some time apart from them. The truth bombs they'd hit her with two weeks ago...about how she'd changed, how weak she'd become... she'd felt blown apart by them.

"You're saying you wish you'd married him?" Peach asked, shocked.

"No, not at all. I just need to learn to trust myself again. To trust my own instincts."

"Instincts that brought you to the Sunshine Trailer Park in Miami?" Kiera asked, wrinkling her nose.

"I'm sorry," Daisy said. "I really can't go back. For starters, I don't want to bump into Raymond for at least a few months. He'll be so angry—"

"Screw him," Kiera interjected. She always had been the fiery one. For someone who made such pretty little bath products, she really did have a temper on her sometimes. "Let him get angry. I'm angry, too. And you should be too for what he did to you."

Daisy shook her head. "I'm not angry. I'm just...disappointed."

In a voice so quiet it was almost a whisper, Peach said, "Well...maybe you should *get* angry."

"No way," Daisy said. "Not my style. I just want to move on. And I *am*. I have a job here now."

"Wait, what?" said Kiera. "A job? Already?" She picked up a glass of the cloudy water on the table, eyed it suspiciously, and put it down again.

"Yeah, I'm working as a PA," Daisy told them. Then, just in case it wasn't clear, she added: "It's a paid position."

She hadn't technically been paid yet, but she'd seen her salary on the contract and it was good. Better than good. Plus, she had health insurance and a pension plan for life. Well, until Montague no doubt fired her one day.

"Well...that's good," Peach said kindly. "Better than all that work you did for free for Raymond. And I'm guessing it pays better than Starbucks."

"Yeah, a little," said Daisy, not wanting to show off. Peach's volunteer job was unpaid and Kiera's company was such a cute idea, but business wasn't exactly booming. Besides, it would be a month before Daisy received her first paycheck. Anything could happen between now and then. She could get fired on the spot, just like the old PA.

Kiera narrowed her eyes. "What kind of company is it? Nothing shady, I hope?"

"No! Of course not!" Daisy protested. "It's just one of those big, boring companies. You know, they just make, like, print cartridges or something."

Print cartridges? Where did that come from?

For some reason, Daisy didn't want to tell the truth about the company— that it was for people involved in the DDlg lifestyle. It was not like her friends would have been judgmental. In fact, they were both Littles too, and the three of them had only ever revealed that secret to each other. And then, of course, Raymond had figured it out, but he had never understood it properly.

Maybe that's why she couldn't tell her friends the truth about Daddies Inc. Because it would seem like she'd betrayed their secret, somehow. After all, it wasn't just her friends that knew her Little secret now. Even her boss knew. Her boss who, as it turned out, was a Daddy Dom. Her boss who, for some reason, had started making her panties melt every time she was close to him. Who—and there was no way she could ever tell her friends this—she was apparently going on some kind of...date...with tonight.

"It sounds boring," said Kiera. "I vote we tie her up and drag her home. What do you say, Peach?"

"Stop it!" Daisy screeched, standing up and knocking over two of the glasses of disgusting trailer water. "Please, just let me live my own life! Let me make my own mistakes!"

Teddy whined, and Daisy felt bad for scaring him. Teddy was a rescue dog and didn't like loud noises.

"Just...go," she said, much more calmly now. "Please."

"All right, all right," said Kiera, raising her hands in surrender. "When you're ready to come home, we'll be waiting for you with a big tub of cookie dough ice cream and a Disney movie." She paused. "You need to grieve for what happened to you, Daisy. Leaving your partner at the altar. Escaping years of abuse. We just want you to process that in a safe way."

"We love you, Daisy," Peach added softly. She made Teddy wave at her again.

A few moments later, her friends had left

And the only sign that they were ever there was the three chipped glasses on the table.

About three seconds after her friends left, the laughing man started his high-pitched giggling again. He must have just woken up.

"Well," she said aloud to the Fairy Godmother on her pillowcase. "At least he had the decency to wait until my friends left."

Friends.

She hoped they still *were* her friends. That meeting hadn't exactly gone great. She just hadn't expected them to turn up in her private space and start lambasting her for trying to start afresh. She needed this break. There was just no way to explain that without making it sound like she was rejecting them. Because, in a way, she *was* rejecting them a little bit. It was only temporary, though. Only until she'd found her own two feet again.

"Speaking of which," she said aloud again, "I need to get ready."

Ready for what exactly? She couldn't say for sure that tonight was a date. What had he called it? An "experiment." She had no idea what that meant. And she had no idea why the moment he'd said it, her panties had become hotter than the sun.

Daisy thought about what getting ready entailed. She'd bought a box of bleach to touch up her roots, but it wasn't going to be that easy without her own shower. She had used the communal shower block once since moving in here, and never again. There was broken glass on the floor, an actual human turd in one of the shower cubicles, no locks on the doors…No thank you very much.

She didn't want to tell her friends, but she'd washed exclusively using the cloudy water in her kitchen sink ever since. At least that water was good for something. She did drink it too, out of necessity, but it tasted like chalky sewer water. Once she got her first paycheck, the first thing she was going to do was start buying bottled water.

"I guess I can wash the dye out over the sink," she told her Fairy Godmother. "Bleach is good for drains anyway, right? Kill two birds with one stone."

As she applied the acrid-smelling bleach to her already strawlike hair, she laughed. "It's funny," she said. "Montague thinks *he's* the one experimenting, but really it's me. Experimenting with living in Miami. Experimenting with working as a PA. Experimenting with spending time with a filthy-rich one-percenter. This is all just a game to me."

She looked into the partially corroded mirror hanging near her sink and smiled at her own reflection.

Every game ends with a winner and a loser, she thought. *Which one will I be?*

CHAPTER 8 - MONTAGUE

This was exactly the kind of romantic occasion that Montague had always shied away from. Dinner under the stars, in a beautiful setting, with a beautiful girl. A Daddy Dom and a Little, sitting opposite one another, seeing where the night would take them.

He knew it was dangerous. He knew nothing was meant to happen between them. He knew that it was an abuse of his position. An abuse of power. An abuse of trust.

He just couldn't help himself.

It had been a long time since he'd let himself be tempted by anything other than money. That was what he was experimenting with tonight: going out for dinner with a gorgeous woman. Seeing whether he had it in him to make her feel special.

Obviously, he wasn't going to try anything untoward. That's not the kind of guy he was. He just wanted an evening with another human being. A connection. And if conversation strayed to work and they ended up tying up a few loose ends from the office, then that was just a bonus.

"I feel a bit out of place," Daisy whispered to Montague, smoothing down her hair with her fingers.

She'd done something to her hair. It looked...dryer than usual. Or lighter. Lighter *and* dryer. Was he supposed to comment on it? *I like how dry your hair looks today?* Maybe not. He was always very blunt with people because he didn't like lies. In fact, to him, lies were just about the worst thing in the entire world.

In spite of the dry hair, though, she looked absolutely radiant. She had a smear of pink lip-gloss on her lips, which seemed to reflect the twinkling light of the stars above them. And she was wearing one of the outfits he'd bought

69

her yesterday morning.

"Nonsense," he said. "You look completely at home here."

"But, sir—"

"You can call me Montague when we're not at work."

Unless we're in a scene. Then you can stick with "Sir." Or "Master."

"Um. Well. Montague it is then," she said, blushing. "I just feel like my pink dress with green frogs all over it isn't necessarily the right look for dining at the former Versace mansion."

Montague didn't smile. He never smiled. In fact, he was deadly serious. "For starters," he said, "that's an extremely elegant dress. It fits your shape perfectly. And who says that frogs aren't sophisticated? For instance, did you know that frogs *drink* through their skin?"

Daisy's jaw dropped. "They what?"

"They don't drink water like we do. They absorb it directly through their skin in an area known as a drinking patch."

"You're making this up."

"I'm not. It's located on their bellies and pelvis."

"They drink water through their pelvis?"

"Yeah," Montague said. "If *that's* not sophisticated, tell me what is." He took a long slurp of water from his glass as if to prove his point.

Daisy giggled. "That's disgusting."

"It's not disgusting," Montague objected. "It's natural. Nature's beautiful." Montague was only now tapping into distant memories from when he was a young boy. As a kid of around seven or eight, he'd loved the natural world. He'd kept tadpoles in jars and had a pet stick insect, and he had been happy playing down by the river for hours on end. Eventually, his dad put a stop to it. Said it was silly and frivolous. Told him he was destined to become a businessman, and it was time to start acting like one.

Daisy looked like she was still considering what he'd just said. "Hmmm. *Fungus* is natural. But it's definitely not beautiful."

Montague didn't want to seem like a know-it-all, so he didn't talk about all the wonderful types of fungus in the world: Orange peel, pixie cup, coral tooth, basket fungi. Everything was beautiful if you knew how to look at it.

"I hope you enjoy the food tonight," he said, changing the subject. "I've heard great things."

"You've never been here before?" Daisy asked, looking around.

"Not to eat," Montague replied. The restaurant in the Versace mansion, Gianni's, was tucked in the Villa Casa Casuarina boutique hotel, which was the old Versace mansion. There was an impressive storied dining room inside the mansion, but there was also an outside seating area by the world-famous mosaic pool, known for its impressive twenty-four gold karat tiles. They had caviar and Champagne at their tables, and an array of wonderful-sounding meals to look forward to, including Kusshi oysters and beef carpaccio.

"What were you doing here then?" asked Daisy.

"Work stuff," said Montague.

Daisy frowned. "You were a chef here? Or a server?"

"Nothing like that." He took a sip of Champagne and encouraged Daisy to do the same. "There are things I haven't explained to you much about Daddies Inc. yet."

"There are?"

"A lot of our clients are of the...older, wealthier persuasion." He ran his fingers through his salt and pepper hair. He wondered if that's how he came across to Daisy. Old. Wealthy. Perhaps *too* old. Too wealthy. "Over the years, the company has built up a strong network of relationships worldwide."

"Right..."

He needed to cut the business jargon. He was making it sound dull. Bastion was better at this stuff than him. He knew how to sell ideas to people. He took a deep breath. "You ever heard of secret menus?"

Daisy smiled and nodded. "I have!"

"Well, Daddies Inc. works with luxury brands across the world to provide secret menus, secret bookings, and secret experiences for Daddies and Littles. It gives them privacy and discretion, but it also allows us to throw in extras for them. Things you wouldn't normally get in a place like this. For example, we throw a pool party for the Littles in that pool over there once a year."

"Right here at the Versace mansion?"

"Yep. Tonight is one of six nights in the year when the only customers allowed to dine here are the private members and customers of Daddies Inc."

"Oh my goodness," said Daisy. "So, like, you have all these secret partnerships with companies all over the world? What other secret menus do you have?"

Montague studied her. "Well, there was the boutique where we went shopping yesterday morning, with the special room at the back. And there are many, many more places. Places which you'll find out about very soon, I'm sure."

Daisy's excited expression suddenly clouded over. "But...there's no-one else here tonight. Is business failing, or something?"

Montague shook his head. "I booked the final two hours just for us."

Daisy put her hand to her mouth. "Can you do that? Didn't that mean a lot of people lost their bookings for tonight?"

"They're staying open an extra two hours for our private booking," Montague explained, sipping his Champagne again.

Daisy looked at him. "That explains the late booking. Don't think I ever ate dinner so late in all my life. I hope I don't fall asleep on you again!" She paused, glancing over at the shimmering gold of the swimming pool, then back at Montague. "I can't even begin to imagine being as rich as you are."

He shrugged. "It comes with its pros and cons."

That's the kind of thing that wealthy people just said, no doubt, but Montague really meant it. The long hours, the stress, the feeling that he'd forgotten how to live. And love.

"How did you get to be so successful?" Daisy asked.

He liked how inquisitive she was. A lot of people would have been embarrassed to quiz him like this. But, in less than three days, she'd become his PA, stayed the night at his house, been shopping with him, and now she was out dining with him. They might not have known one another for a long time, but a bond was forming. It felt good.

"If I'm being honest," he told her, "I got this way through being extremely

72

cutthroat. My father taught me how. On my eighteenth birthday, he gave me a ten-dollar bill. Told me to make it into a thousand dollars by the end of the year, otherwise I'd be out on my ass. Unfortunately, I bought stock in a company that started to plummet in value almost the day after I invested. My dad threw me out, just like he'd promised.

"That's terrible."

"It was harsh...but it taught me to be more careful with my money. I decided to hell with investing in other people's companies, and set up my own there and then."

"You set up Daddies Inc. at the age of eighteen?"

"Hell no," Montague replied. "I barely knew how to tie my own shoelaces when I was eighteen. I certainly didn't know I was a Daddy Dom."

Those words hung in the air between them. Had he been too straight with her? It felt strangely good to get it out in the open. It's not like he was embarrassed of who he was. He just felt...vulnerable, which was something he wasn't used to feeling.

"Anyway," he said, "the company was kind of dull. I noticed a gap in the market for a good packing box company in the Midwest. So I started one. And after that, everything kind of exploded. Isaac was one of my early investors, and we made a ton of money. The company's still going, but Isaac wanted something more. And so did Bastion, who first made his money in the oil industry."

"But when did the three of you realize you were all Daddies?"

"That wasn't until we'd started our third company. We took a trip to New York. It was around the time I turned thirty. We were headed for a conference on entrepreneurship. Steve Jobs was one of the speakers. Anyway, we arrived the night before and we had some time to kill. We headed to a nearby fetish club kind of as a joke, but it ended up becoming something much more serious for all of us."

"You discovered that you were Daddies there?"

"We discovered that we were Doms, that's for sure. Each of us had our own private experiences that night, but we came to the same conclusion. And when Isaac shared something that he had done in the age play room, his story resonated with all of us. It wasn't long before we were all practicing Daddy Doms. And only two years after that, Daddies Inc. was born. It was my idea. Guess I got sick of feeling like I had to confine my lifestyle to fetish clubs. I wanted to be able to do normal stuff as a Daddy Dom."

"Normal stuff like...hanging out at the Versace mansion?" Daisy inquired with a smirk.

Montague decided not to rise to the bait and continued with his explanation. "The idea behind Daddies Inc. is that it's creating a world where Daddies and Littles can experience anything they want without judgment. Sure, we provide high-end experiences. Luxury villas, designer shopping labels, Michelin-star restaurants, and so on. But that's because we're working with what we know. Our philosophy is simple, though. No one should have to hide because they like to connect with their inner child, or dole out a few spanks from time to time. Love is love, as long as it's safe, sane, and consensual."

Daisy whistled. "Now *that's* beautiful."

"You're beautiful," Montague blurted before he could stop himself.

Luckily, the food arrived just as he'd said that, distracting her from his clumsy compliment.

"This looks amazing. Thank you." She paused. "You know, I really would never have guessed in a million years that we'd be doing *this* together when I first met you three days ago."

Those words stung Montague a little. Did he come across as that unlikeable? "Tell me honestly," he said to her. "What do you really think of me?"

Daisy chewed thoughtfully on some beef carpaccio, momentarily distracted by how delicious it was. "I guess you can be a little mean," she said at last. "As much as I'm grateful to have this job, I feel like..."

"Go on," he urged her.

"Firing your old PA was pretty unfair. Linda seemed nice."

"She tried to poison me."

Daisy looked away.

74

"What? What is it?" he said. "You look like you're hiding something from me."

"Well, I spoke to some of the staff about what happened. They told me someone had stuck the wrong label over the cashew milk by mistake. It wasn't Linda's fault."

"Whose fault was it?" Montague asked, his spine stiffening. "Did you get a name?"

"No," Daisy replied. "See, that's the thing. It seems like it was an honest mistake. I don't think people feel too comfortable coming forward and telling the truth in case they're punished for it."

Montague felt his smartwatch pulse three times, and he knew that meant he needed to slow his heart rate down. He counted backward from five and slowed his breath. "You're right. The office should be a safe space. People should feel comfortable to speak their truths." He closed his eyes. "I've always struggled with keeping a lid on my bad moods, ever since I was a kid. But the past few months have been the worst."

"How come?" Daisy asked. "Did something happen?"

He didn't want to talk about his wife. He wasn't ready to open that can of particularly unpleasant worms yet. Maybe he never would be. "My father died of a heart attack three months ago. It's one of the reasons I've been so snippy."

Daisy put down her cutlery. "I'm so sorry. Were you close?"

"Close like a ball and chain," he replied. "You heard what he did when I was eighteen. He only got less kind as he grew older."

"That must be hard. Feeling angry with him, but having nowhere for that anger to go."

He nodded, feeling strangely seen. She seemed to have figured out his deal so fast, and already it felt like she got him better than Bastion or Isaac. "So, tell me about *yourself*, little mouse," he said, again changing the subject. "What makes Daisy Grove tick?"

"Oh, the usual," she said. "Sunshine. Adventure. Romance."

"No suppressed anger with nowhere to go?" he joked.

She paused. "Nope. Not me. No, siree."

"What brought you to Miami?" he asked. "You don't have the accent. I'm guessing you're from someplace up north originally. You running away from something?"

Daisy looked at him wide-eyed. "Me? Nah. Just wanted to catch some sun. And check out Dade-D Bar."

"That's cute," he replied. "You came all that way to visit one of my bars?"

She seemed surprised. "That's a Daddies Inc. bar?"

"Of course."

"Wow, you really do have your fingers in all the pies." She gulped down an oyster in one swallow, then grinned. "But I didn't come all this way *just* for that bar. I wanted an adventure."

"An adventure, huh?"

"Never really had the chance for an adventure before. Figured I deserved one."

"We all deserve a little adventure from time to time."

Daisy paused. "I wanted to see how I coped on my own, without my old friends. To try to make some new ones. To find work. To find my own two feet. And, er, I also wanted to be near Disney World. I guess I'm toying with trying to get a job *there* eventually."

He leaned forward, intrigued. "PA to Mickey Mouse?"

"No." She shook her head. "I always wanted to play Cinderella."

"Interesting." He checked his watch. "Uh oh."

"What?" she asked, concerned.

"It's quarter to midnight," he replied. "I'd better get you home soon, Cinders."

CHAPTER 9 - DAISY

Daisy felt like she was in a music video for the song "Walking on Sunshine." She skipped down the sidewalk on the way to work, high-fived a kid *and* a kid's mom, and at one point, she even jumped for joy.

It didn't matter that the laughing man had kept her awake most of last night. It didn't matter that she'd woken up in her trailer to find the water had stopped working. And it didn't matter that she hadn't been able to afford anything to eat yesterday, and she had to walk all the way to work this morning because she couldn't afford the bus fare.

Saturday night had been a fairy-tale. The glitz of the Versace mansion, the elaborate frescoes, the glimmering tiles, the insanely delicious food. And Montague opposite her: attentive, encouraging, and even cracking the occasional joke. Plus, and this hadn't gone unnoticed, he'd called her beautiful. Maybe he was just being polite. Maybe he had been a little drunk. Maybe he'd gotten carried away with the glamor of the setting.

Who cared?

That night, for one night only, Daisy had felt like a princess. All her years dating Raymond and she hadn't felt like that once. It had felt amazing to visit that magical place, to live like royalty, just once in her life. Even if it never happened again, it had happened once, and she could live off those memories for the rest of her life.

As it turned out, the evening had ended kind of abruptly. There was no way after an evening like that that Daisy could have revealed her trailer park address to Montague. So, after they left the mansion, when Montague had offered to have his driver take her back, she'd simply yelled, "No, it's okay thanks! Gotta run!" And she'd turned on her heel and jogged away.

Still, even that awkward exit hadn't spoiled the evening. For her, at least.

And luckily, unlike *Cinderella*, she hadn't lost a shoe as she'd jogged away. Five minutes later, puffing and panting, she'd hailed down a cab to take her back. A cab that had cost her so much it had bled her bank account dry.

Not to worry. This morning, she was heading to work to do her important job that would help people and earn her money. Maybe, in time, the people in the office would stop hating her so much too. But hey, one thing at a time.

As she glided down the sidewalk, she thought about that word some more. *Beautiful.*

Nobody had ever called her that. Raymond sometimes called her "delicious" and "good enough to eat", which always felt oddly predatory coming from him. Considering he was a novelist, she didn't think much of his word choices. Montague's were much better.

Just before she arrived at work, her phone buzzed. She wondered if Montague was texting her. A little reminder of something that had occurred between them at the weekend. An in-joke about froggy "drinking patches", maybe. Or the photo he'd taken of her balancing an oyster shell on her head.

But when she saw who it was, her empty stomach lurched.

Raymond.

She didn't want to read the message, but she had to. It was the first one he'd sent her since she'd abandoned him at the altar. She had to at least see what he had to say for himself.

Daisy, I'm sorry I never appreciated you. I deserved what happened. I want another chance. Love you, sexy mama.

Daisy read and re-read the message. It was weird. It didn't sound like Raymond. She had been expecting it to be cruel, or vindictive. This message sounded respectful, apologetic, all the things that Raymond wasn't.

She realized as she read those words, "love you", that she'd never really felt true love herself. That was one of the reasons she'd been so sure that she had to leave him. She was a romantic, it was true. And sometimes, because of that, she'd tried to persuade herself that what she felt for Raymond was love. But it never even came close. It was more like...habit. Hope.

She looked at the text message again, shuddering at the phrase "sexy mama"...he'd never called her that. She wasn't sure what she disliked worse—being called that, or "delicious". It just wasn't *her*. For one thing, she was a Little. Definitely not a *mama*. But then, Raymond had never really gotten that about her. He'd always called her childish when she played with toys, or cuddled stuffies. Forced her to wear drab jeans and sweaters around him because he told her the bright, fun clothes she wore were "embarrassing." One of the most hurtful things he'd said was: "All this Little stuff is just an excuse for you to never accept any adult responsibility." So, Daisy had only ever let her true Little out around her best friends, which was draining, to say the least.

Never mind. Raymond was in the past now. She wasn't going to be won back with a text message, that was for sure. She was finally *free*. She had a real job. And a real boss who was a real man. A bit of a grump, sure, but she'd take a grump over a gaslighter any day of the week.

She walked through the sliding doors of the impressive office block she worked in, sighing with pleasure at the feeling of the cool air inside the building. She greeted Brock, the tattooed security guy who worked at the door, and she took the elevator up to the seventh floor. When the elevator doors opened, she frowned.

"Oops." She must have punched in the wrong number, because this wasn't her floor.

She turned to the elevator console, but sure enough, the number seven was lit up. She stepped out, puzzled. This place had completely changed over the weekend.

"Morning, Daisy!" called out one of her colleagues, Scotia.

Daisy was even more puzzled. Scotia had *definitely* given her the side-eye on Friday, and Daisy was pretty sure she'd heard her whispering something nasty about her hair, too. Ah well. She returned Scotia's greeting and gave her a warm smile. Life was too short to hold grudges.

As she continued to walk toward her desk, she began to wonder: was it possible that she'd stepped into a parallel universe? A universe where her workplace had happy staff, a jungle gym, a trampoline, an art area, a nap corner, and...*a juice station*!

Oh my goodness. This was all too good to be true. Montague and Sam and the others had really listened to her. And not just listened to her—they'd implemented everything she'd suggested *and then some*.

"Wow," she said aloud. "This is just...wow."

"Good morning, little mouse," a deep voice said into her ear. "What do you think of the changes around here?"

Daisy turned to look at her boss, and she swore that *he* looked different too. Younger, somehow. Not like any creepy transformation had taken place, but just...more relaxed, less lined around the eyes and mouth, less uptight.

"It's amazing," she breathed. "I only sent the email through yesterday morning. It's like a completely different workplace!"

"You can get things done fast if you know the right people," Montague replied. "One of the companies we partner with specializes in interior design for Littles."

Daisy shook her head, still hardly able to believe her eyes. "It's like I've witnessed some kind of miracle."

"Well, the surprises don't end there," he said. "Follow me."

Daisy had no idea what her boss was about to show her. All kinds of crazy ideas ran through her mind. A swimming pool? A climbing wall? A petting zoo?

"Linda's back," said Montague, stopping abruptly in front of a lime green desk.

Daisy stood in front of Linda, taken aback. Here was the woman whose job she'd taken. Would Linda be mad at her? If Montague had taken her back, did this mean that Daisy was out of a job again?

"It's okay," Montague said, looking at her and sensing her worry. "Linda and I had a long chat yesterday, didn't we?"

Linda nodded and smiled. "We sure did, boss."

"I explained to Linda that I've been under a lot of pressure lately. That I haven't been myself for some months now."

Linda leaned over her desk. "He apologized for being an asshole," she said quietly, giving Daisy a conspiratorial wink. "His words, not mine.

Although..."

Daisy giggled. "Well, I'm glad you're back, Linda."

"From what Montague told me, I have *you* to thank for it," Linda replied.

Daisy shrugged, bashful. "Oh, it was nothing."

"Linda is taking on a new role within the company," Montague explained. "She's going to be our Office Manager from now on."

Daisy chewed on the inside of her lip thoughtfully. "So...is that different than a PA?"

"Totally," Linda replied. "I get to play to my strengths in the new role. Nurturing the staff. Making sure the art supplies are fully stocked, that the nap corner is comfortable, and everyone is feeling fresh and cared for."

"Linda and I agreed that it's well-suited to her Mommy side," Montague added.

Linda didn't seem in the least bit embarrassed by that comment. In fact, she appeared to like it. She adjusted her shiny gold spectacles, nodding.

"Oh, also, I bought Linda some spectacles," Montague added. "Turned out, she'd started to need glasses. Should help us avoid any issues with products having the wrong labels in the future, right, Linda?"

"Absolutely, boss," said Linda. "Plus, we've banned nuts from the office. Better to be safe than sorry."

"I'm trying to go easy on the rules," said Montague. "But that does seem like a good one."

Linda beamed at them both.

Montague led Daisy away from Linda, who gave an enthusiastic wave as they walked away. "I really can't thank you enough for your ideas."

"It's really not that big of a deal," said Daisy, fiddling with her blouse sleeves out of embarrassment.

"You like to do that, huh?" said Montague. "You like to minimize your own achievements."

"I guess it's good to be humble."

"That's true," Montague replied. "But it's also important to allow yourself to feel a sense of accomplishment. You did good, Daisy Grove. So, whaddya say? You gonna let me pour you a glass of celebratory juice?"

Daisy laughed. "Okay."

They walked over to the juice station, and several more members of staff greeted Daisy along the way. She felt awkward about getting all this attention from her boss. She didn't want to be the teacher's pet or anything. She'd only been here five minutes.

At the same time, she was loving all this one-on-one time with Montague. She kept thinking back to their date together at the weekend. To him calling her beautiful. She felt as though they shared a secret, and it gave every moment between them a special kind of frisson. Like there was electricity crackling along invisible wires between the two of them.

Montague poured her an orange juice. "This is the best," he told her, "because it's freshly squeezed. Valencia oranges from a farm just south of here. Delicious."

Daisy took the juice and gulped it down gratefully. This was the first drink she'd had today. It was her breakfast, too.

"Thirsty, huh?" Montague observed.

Daisy was about to reply, but her rumbling tummy answered for her.

"Hungry as well? You'd better head to our snack wagon."

"Snack wagon?"

Montague pointed it out to her, just across from the juice station.

It was amazing. Even from where she stood, she could see rice cakes. Fruit. Veggie straws. Oat and blueberry muffins.

"I can really help myself to anything I want?"

"Sure," Montague replied. "As much as you like, whenever you like. It's all healthy."

Daisy felt a rush of emotion. This was all so incredible. But she didn't deserve it. All this lovely stuff. The juice station, the Versace mansion, the praise from her coworkers.

"I...I'm not a real PA," she whispered, her voice cracking.

Montague frowned. "Pardon?"

Oh god. Why did I do that? Do I have a death wish or something?

CHAPTER 9 - DAISY

She felt weak, like her knees were buckling, and the room was spinning.

"I-I'm not a real PA, Mr. Manners. I lied to get the job. I was never a copywriter, either. Unless you count coming up with the name 'Fizz Pop' for a bubble bath company."

Montague narrowed his eyes at her. In a low voice, being careful not to let anyone else hear the conversation, he said, "You told me in your interview that you'd worked for an author."

"I did. I mean, nothing I said was a lie exactly. I just made it sound more impressive than it was." Tears filled her eyes. "Nothing I've ever done has been impressive. I'm so sorry. I've wasted your time. The author I told you about was just my ex-boyfriend. He expected me to do a lot of work for him for free, and he treated me like trash."

Montague's expression clouded over. "You'd better come to my office right now."

Daisy swallowed. "Now?"

She looked wistfully at the blueberry muffins. She had at least hoped she'd get to enjoy some of the free food before she lost this job. She had no money, after all. No food. No water. No plan.

Sorrowfully, she followed Montague to his office. Once they were inside, he closed the blinds.

"Sit there, young lady," he said, pointing to a shiny wooden chair shaped like a giant hand.

Wait. Was that thing there last time she was in here? No. She'd have noticed it.

"I thought I'd treat myself," Montague said, noticing that Daisy was looking at it. "With all the changes around here, it felt like my office needed a little attention too. So I brought my favorite chair out of storage."

Montague's office was perfect. Always had been. But the hand chair certainly gave it a quirky appeal.

"It's a Pedro Friedeberg original," he said. "Crafted in Mexican mahogany. Marvelous, don't you think?"

"It's something else," Daisy agreed, sitting delicately in the palm of the hand. It felt surprisingly comfortable. Even rather grounding. Like she was being held securely by Planet Earth itself. She'd have felt strangely at peace if it wasn't for the fact she felt sure she was about to be fired.

She took a deep breath, trying to calm herself. She had to tell the truth back there. She just had to. All this fuss, all these congratulations. She was starting to feel like a fake. She couldn't have lived with that.

Montague perched on the edge of his desk, looking down at her. "Daisy," he said at last, "what makes you think that you don't deserve good things?"

Daisy hesitated. She hadn't been expecting that question. She had been expecting something angrier. Something more abrupt. Something involving the word "fired."

"Um...I d-don't know," she stammered. "I guess I never really thought about myself like that before."

"You told me out there that you don't deserve this job. You told me that your ex treated you like trash. It seems that there's a pattern here. Bad things happen to you, and you endure them because you feel like that's all you're worth. Good things happen, and you try to self-sabotage because you don't feel worthy."

"I g-guess," said Daisy.

"So what I'm wondering," Montague asked, "is did something happen to you to make you that way? Were you ever bullied, Daisy?"

She hadn't been expecting *that* question either. She thought back to her childhood. Getting bullied by her stepmom for being an inconvenience. Getting bullied by the other kids at school for wearing glasses. More recently, being bullied by Raymond for being childish.

Slowly, Daisy nodded. "Yeah. I was. For wearing glasses, among other things."

Montague nodded, scratching the designer stubble on his chin thoughtfully. He looked as though he was trying to figure out the best way to approach something, but Daisy couldn't figure out what on earth it could be.

Finally, he set his jaw resolutely, and then looked straight at her. "If you were my Little," he said, "I'd spank your ass for saying nasty things about yourself."

She sniffed. "You should be mad at me for lying."

Montague shook his head. "Sweetheart, you didn't lie. Your resumé did exactly what a resumé *should* do. It bigged you up. With extra glitter."

She smiled weakly.

"So what if you just made up some funny names for a bubble bath company? That's still important work. So what if your previous boss was your ex-boyfriend? It was still work. You didn't lie about any of it."

Daisy's heart skipped a beat. Her previous boss *was* her ex-boyfriend. Was there any way that her current boss could be her current boyfriend?

She decided to take a chance.

"Boss," she said quietly, "do you really think getting spanked would help me?" She fidgeted on the chair, on the giant hand that was cupping her ass.

"Undoubtedly," he said. "Though it might take a few sessions before you started to make a deep association between putting yourself down and getting spanked." He paused. "And also, someone with a disposition like yours would require a lot of aftercare."

"What's my disposition like?" Daisy asked, her breath growing jagged.

"You're a fighter," he said. "Strong as an ox. I can see that. You've been through a ton. I bet I only know the half of it. But that makes you fragile, too. Your toughness is only an outer shell, designed to protect your fragile core. You need careful handling, my girl, or you'll crack."

Daisy nodded, running her eyes over her boss, starting with his salt and pepper hair, and traveling down over his wide torso, his groin, his muscular thighs. Carefully, making her words creep out as softly as if on tiptoes, she said: "I think you're a very good Daddy."

Montague's body stiffened, just a touch, but enough for Daisy to know that he'd been affected by her words.

Daisy waited, not wanting to push things any further. It was up to him now. She hoped that she'd made herself clear.

Montague glanced up at the closed blinds and then looked back at Daisy. "If you like," he said, "I'll show you exactly what kind of Daddy I am."

Daisy nodded. "Yes, please."

Montague's expression changed. It became steely. Dark. Sure. "Pull down your pants then, babygirl," he said. "And bend over that chair."

CHAPTER 10 - MONTAGUE

Montague had seen some awe-inspiring sights in his time. He'd seen the lagoons of Polynesia, the Rainbow Mountains of China, and the sand dunes of Namibia. He'd lived a life of freedom, indulgence, and pure delight.

And yet nothing—*nothing*—compared to the sight of Daisy's bare white ass, bent over his favorite chair, waiting for his palm to make contact. She'd pulled down her leggings, just as he'd asked. Now, she was holding on tightly to the fingers on the back of the chair, her ass sticking out just for him.

He loved every curve of her. Every dimple and contour seemed to have been specifically designed to please him. It was like looking at the artwork of a master craftsman.

The pleasure wasn't just visual, either. He felt honored that this wonderful woman trusted him enough to do this. They didn't yet have a contract. They hadn't known each other for long. What was happening between them was clearly taking both of them by surprise. And undoubtedly breaching some important office policies.

And yet here she was. In her boss's office, with her panties down, showing him one of her most intimate places.

"Daddy's very proud of you for being such a good girl and taking your spanking," he told her.

He knew that they were just roleplaying. He wasn't officially her Daddy yet. But he'd like to be. So what if he was her boss? Hearing that her ex had been her boss too made him feel more open to the idea. If other people in the office found it a little unconventional, well...screw them. Everything about Daddies Inc. was unconventional. Convention was overrated.

"I'm going to deliver ten smacks. You may find that the smacks start to sting more as they go on. That's perfectly normal, and it just shows that the spanks are effective. But if it gets too much at any time, then use a safeword of your choice and I will stop immediately and move straight to aftercare."

"Bibbity-bobbity-boo," said Daisy.

What?

"That's my safeword," she added.

"All right," said Montague. "*Flibberty-jibbity-whatever-it-was* it is."

"*Bibbity-bobbity-boo*," Daisy said insistently.

"Got it," Montague said. "Bibbity-babbity-boop."

"That's almost right, Daddy," Daisy replied with a giggle.

"I'd like you to refer to me as 'sir' for the duration of the spanking," said Montague. "Then, during the aftercare, we can revert back to Daddy. Once that is finished, I'm afraid, for the remainder of the working day, you'll refer to me as 'boss.'"

"Not a problem, sir," she answered brightly.

He could tell she was as excited by this as he was. Hell, she had practically instigated this whole thing. Or at least, she'd made it very clear that she was into the idea.

"Here we go," he said. "Ten smacks starting now."

Montague lifted back his palm and slapped Daisy right in the middle of her ass cheeks, causing them to wobble. Her flesh felt incredible under his hand. So warm and soft, like dough. He was tempted to forget the smacks and just play around with her ass for a while, but he knew that he couldn't. He had a job to do.

"While I deliver these spanks, Daisy, I want you to think about how naughty it is to talk badly about yourself. Each and every smack is a reminder not to insult the person that should be most important to you: yourself."

"Yes, sir," Daisy said obediently. She wasn't fooling around anymore. This was serious.

He spanked her again, harder now. Again, he had to force himself to take his hand away from her peachy ass. He was desperate to move his palm down a little farther, to explore the pussy lips that he could just about make out poking out from between her thighs. He wondered how wet she was right now. He wondered whether she'd ever been spanked like this before. He wondered how it would feel to fuck her while he spanked her. He wondered, wondered, wondered.

Slap.

His cock thickened in his pants as his hand rained down on her. If he hadn't been at work, he'd have quite happily released his hard-on and jerked off while he spanked her. He was so turned on right now—so desperate for her —that if he'd let himself, he was pretty sure he'd have shot his load all over her ass by the time he reached number ten.

Slap. Slap. Slap.

He didn't pander to his cock's attempts at distraction. Instead, he got the job done. He watched her ass turn from white to blush, from blush to peach and from peach to cherry. Hot damn, he'd missed this. Guiding a woman with his firm hand. The power dynamic. The dark, insatiable lust. The deep, unrivaled connection.

When the smacks were over, he instructed Daisy to sit back down on the hand, keeping her pants around her ankles. She winced a little as she sat on the chair, but fortunately, the smooth wood seemed to cradle and caress her ass, and after a few moments, her pained expression eased.

"Sweetheart," he said. "Daddy's proud of you. So very proud." He kneeled before her, enveloping her in his arms. "You took every single spank so well."

"Thank you, Daddy," said Daisy, nuzzling into his shoulder. "I was a bit scared to start off with, but I feel as though it's helped me. I'm determined not to put myself down anymore."

"It's all right if you make mistakes, Little one," he said. "Learning is a process. It takes time." He stroked her thighs as he sat before her, then gently pulled her thighs apart from one another. "Daddy would like to give you a special kiss now," he said, looking longingly at her pussy, which was even pinker than her ass. A beautiful shade. He was thrilled to see how moist she was, too. Wet, and open, and ready for him. "I want to remind you just how wonderful you are."

Daisy nodded trustingly. "Okay, Daddy."

His heart melted for her. She was so right for him. So sweet, so submissive, so...Daisy.

As his face nestled between her thighs, his smartwatch began to pulse. Probably telling him that he was getting excited and needed to take a breather. Well, there was just no way. He was diving in, headfirst, and never coming out ever again. His mouth moved close to her pussy lips. He could smell her sweet, salty scent. He could feel her velvet-smoothness on his lips.

"Um, boss?" said Daisy.

Uh oh.

He didn't like that. She'd called him "boss", not "Daddy." Something was up.

"What is it, sweetie?" he asked, looking up at her.

"My phone just buzzed," she said. "It's time for our ten o'clock meeting."

Shit.

How was it that time already?

Now it made sense. *That's* what his smartwatch had been trying to communicate to him. Well, fuck, fuck, fuck. His whole life long, he'd escaped into his work whenever he wanted to feel happy. Now, all he wanted to do was escape from work between Daisy's thighs.

"Are you angry, boss?" asked Daisy warily. "Should I have warned you about it earlier?"

"No, little mouse," said Montague, pressing his forefinger gently on the tip of his nose. "I'm very glad that you didn't. I'm just not happy about leaving things...like this." He looked down at her pussy, which was wetter than ever for him. The poor little thing had been anticipating his touch. Now, it would be dripping wet throughout the entire meeting. Not to mention his cock would be hard as rock.

"It's all right, sir," said Daisy. "I had a good time. But it had to end sooner or later." She smiled sadly. "Every fairytale must come to an end."

Montague frowned. "Nobody's talking about endings yet, are they?"

Daisy's expression brightened and she shook her head.

"And by the way," he told her, "you don't have to call me 'sir' when it's

90

just the two of us like this. Not unless we're in a scene. Spanking or...sex."

"Oh. I'm sorry. I guess I got confused, boss."

"You don't have to call me boss, either," he said. "Not when we're in private."

"So, what should I call you then?" asked Daisy. "Mr. Manners?"

"No," he said with certainty. "You can call me 'Daddy'."

Daisy nodded, and a wide grin spread across her face. "Okay, Daddy."

He noticed that she was still sitting with her legs wide apart, her pussy leaving beautiful glistening patterns all over his chair. He knew what that meant. This work meeting was not a stop button. They were simply leaving things on pause.

He couldn't take his damn eyes off her. He knew from the way she fidgeted in her seat that her ass was uncomfortable, and the rosiness of her cheeks reminded him constantly of the redness of her ass.

Under the table, his cock was straining to get to her. He listened to the things his colleagues were saying as well as he could but his cock was shouting, *screaming*, for pussy. And it wasn't just his cock. Every part of his body was alive with wanting her. His palm tingled from slapping her butt. His lips had barely grazed her pussy, but somehow her taste was all over his tongue.

She was acting completely professional, of course. She hid behind those fun yellow glasses, writing notes and stopping now and then to studiously bite her pencil while she listened. But he knew that no matter how hard she was trying to appear unaffected by the spanking, her pussy would still be soaking her panties right now.

"Montague? Hello, Montague?" Bastion waved his hand in front of Montague's face. "Earth to Montague."

"Sorry," Montague said, shaking his head. "I was a million miles away."

Not entirely true. I was mere inches away. Completely distracted by the thought of my PA's soaking wet pussy.

"Try to keep up," Bastion said. "We're talking about the gnome trail in the Botanical Gardens. We've been offered exclusive access for a night while the trail is taking place. Not exactly a luxury experience, but sure to be a hit with the Littles. We could make an evening of it. A summer barbecue, classical music, a rare plant auction. What do you think?"

"Sounds good," Montague said, still thinking about Daisy's pussy. "Sounds very, very good."

"Great," said Bastion. "I'll get the paperwork together."

"How's the theme park idea coming along?" Isaac interjected.

"Great," Montague replied, trying to force himself to come back into the room.

"How much of a budget are you thinking about allocating?" Isaac asked.

"Not sure yet."

"Remember to keep me up to speed," Isaac said.

Montague nodded. Good old Isaac. Always on top of the finances. If it hadn't been for his mathematical genius, this company wouldn't have had half the success it had enjoyed.

Suddenly, a thought occurred to Montague. "I need to do some research. Can't build a theme park without checking out the competition now, can I?"

Bastion laughed. "Montague Manners, the grumpiest man I know, wants to visit a theme park?"

"Not just any theme park," Montague said. "I want to go to the best theme park on the planet: Disney World. And I'll need to take my PA."

Daisy looked at him. Her jaw dropped.

"Absolutely not," Bastion replied. But, after a pause, he said: "it would make much more sense to go to Disneyland *Paris*. We have that deal with the Eiffel Tower that needs firming up, so you might as well tackle both things at once."

Montague was pleasantly surprised. Maybe Bastion was growing soft in his old age. Trying to be as subtle as he could, he looked over at Daisy and raised his eyebrows questioningly.

Stifling a smile, Daisy nodded her head slightly.

CHAPTER 10 - MONTAGUE

"Fine," Montague agreed. "Disneyland Paris it is."

They finished up the meeting shortly after that, but Montague was barely listening. All he could think about was Daisy Grove. Taking an airplane with her. Staying at a hotel with her. Walking around Paris with her. Eating her pussy, day and night, whenever he felt like it.

As he walked out of the meeting room, he reminded himself to hold his clipboard over his groin, just like he'd had to do on the way in.

"I can't believe you suggested that," Daisy hissed to him as they walked back toward his office.

"Want to celebrate in the hand chair?" he asked her, pressing that clipboard harder than ever against his crotch.

"Y—"

Daisy's words were interrupted by Scotia, asking if she could "borrow" her for a minute.

Shit. Of course Scotia could borrow her. This was *work*, not a goddamn dirty weekend.

But he was going book tickets for Paris tomorrow. And it would be the dirtiest fucking *week* of their lives.

CHAPTER 11 - DAISY

———————

Daisy's head was in the clouds. Literally and figuratively.

She couldn't believe it: she'd been in her job less than a week and already she'd somehow changed the entire workplace, stayed over at her boss' house, gone on a date with him, gotten seriously naughty with him in the office, and now she was going on vacation with him.

Okay, okay, it was *work*, technically, and not a vacation. But what difference did that make? Her boss was her Daddy and her Daddy was her boss. So whether it was work or a vacation, the outcome was the same. Her tingly places were going to get some serious attention!

She looked out the airplane window, thinking about what had happened between them just twenty-four hours ago. She'd loved every second of it. Baring herself for him. Getting spanked. Getting *almost* licked.

It had been a real bummer that he hadn't been able to finish that job. She'd always felt self-conscious about oral sex, but somehow it was different with him. How could she be with the way he looked at her? She could tell how into it he was. But there had been something exciting about having to stop for the meeting, too. Her knickers had been so wet when she went to the bathroom afterward she'd been worried about her leggings having a damp patch on them, but luckily they were fine.

Obviously, she'd hoped they could have finished what they'd started yesterday, but there seemed to be a million things to do at the office, and honestly, it was probably for the best. She needed to get to know the staff members, and she had all sorts of important stuff to learn from Linda: how the filing system worked, how to use the intercom system, and so on.

By the end of the day, her head was buzzing with lust and new information, and it had been such a downer to head back to the trailer. Montague had been stuck in a meeting with a client, otherwise she might have stayed behind to see him, but no such luck. She'd had to go back to reality. No food, no water, and incessant creepy laughter until three in the morning.

But so what? She was here now, flying business class across the Atlantic Ocean for the first time in her life with an older man who seemed, for some reason, to genuinely care about her.

"You want a glass of water?" Montague asked her as the steward passed by.

"I'd rather have one of those mini gin and tonic cans," said Daisy. "They're soooo cute!"

Montague had already told her the trip was all expenses paid. Whatever she wanted, she could have it. Except, it seemed, a teeny tiny can of gin and tonic.

"Nuh-uh," he said, keeping his eyes fixed on a boring work report he was reading. "The humidity in here is lower than in the desert. Eight hours up here and you'll suffer dehydration if you're not careful. Plus, there's the decreased pressure of the flight cabin, which reduces your body's ability to absorb oxygen. That could make you feel much drunker, even after a tiny can of alcohol."

Daisy *humphed* quietly. She didn't want to cause trouble with her boss, so she didn't get bratty or anything.

At least it sounded like Montague was looking out for her. She didn't like the sound of getting dehydrated and overly drunk, that was for sure.

It still hurt, though. She guessed she was just a little sensitive about being told that she couldn't do things. Raymond had always been so controlling. *Don't wear this, don't do that, don't talk to him, don't look over there.* There was a difference between bossiness and boundaries, though. Raymond had stopped Daisy from living her life for selfish reasons. Montague let her know his reasons for not allowing her to drink on the plane, and his reasons were sensible and in her best interests. She guessed the transition would take some getting used to. She'd never had a Daddy before—only a dick.

She snickered at the thought, but Montague didn't look up. Dang it. He was completely absorbed in that boring report. Just a bunch of pie charts, each one dryer than the last. Dry, dry, dry. Was there anything worse than dry pie?

"As you know, there will be a lot to fit in while we're here," Montague said to her, turning the page of his report to reveal—*Woah! It's a miracle!*—another pie chart. "Daddies Inc. is running a romantic getaway for DDlgs in Paris next spring. We're looking to partner with the Eiffel Tower for the night, but I'd like to check out a few other possible venues as well. Théâtre Chochotte, for example, which is a bohemian spot in the sixth *arrondissement*. A cross between a cabaret, an art exhibition, and a strip club."

Daisy's heart sank a little. He wanted to go to a strip club. Wasn't she enough for him? The spanking. The spark. Was it all over now?

Montague put down his report and looked at her. "What is it, little mouse?"

"It's nothing," Daisy said, her lip trembling.

Montague narrowed his eyes. "It doesn't look like nothing. You're feeling...nervous? Disappointed? Afraid?"

"I'm not afraid," Daisy said, shaking her head. "Not at all. It's just...when you suggested the trip to Disney World yesterday, I thought—I *hoped*—that it was so that you and I could get some alone time. But if we're going to be running around a million venues, including strip clubs—"

"Daisy," Montague interrupted her softly, "this whole trip is about us. We're going to spend five nights here. Two full days to explore Disneyland, and then two days exploring some of the most romantic–and sexy–places Paris has to offer." He paused, leaning in toward her. "You know, the strip club I just mentioned is extremely forward-thinking. No taboos in a place like that. They *encourage* audience participation. If we wanted to, we could fuck right there, in the audience, and we'd become part of the show."

Daisy giggled. She appreciated Montague trying to cheer her up, but she didn't want to be part of any show. She just wanted to be *his*.

"You're going to love Paris," Montague insisted, squeezing her hand, sending electricity all the way up her arm. "And of course I'm not honestly suggesting we fuck in every venue we visit. Although..." He looked at her longingly. "I could be persuaded."

Daisy blushed. A wicked smile spread across her lips. "Even in this airplane?"

Montague looked at her sternly. "You heard what I said about the air pressure in here. That would be a terrible idea."

"Sorry, Daddy," Daisy said. "I was just being silly."

"Well, every time you're silly," he whispered into your ear, "it makes my cock a little bit harder. So behave yourself, young lady."

Daisy nodded, feeling herself get instantly wetter. "I promise to never be silly again, Daddy," she whispered back. "It would be very, very bad if your Daddy-bits got hard. Especially when my Little-bits are so wet. Anything could happen when we get to Paris. And I mean *anything*."

Montague made a noise.

She swore it was a growl.

The Plaza Athénée was no ordinary hotel. Situated on the Champs-Élysées, the famous avenue of designer shops like Louis Vuitton, Chanel, Givenchy, and Prada, it had the most stunning view over some of the most iconic landmarks of Paris—including, of course, the Eiffel Tower. It had an indoor courtyard covered in beautiful red geraniums, five different restaurants, a luxury spa...the list went on.

Unfortunately, she and Montague had separate rooms. She had known that was the case, though, since he'd asked her to book the rooms at work yesterday. One room would have set the alarm bells ringing among other staff members immediately. Besides, Montague was a gentleman and wanted to give her the option of her own space.

Montague had the Presidential Suite, obviously. The most luxurious spot in the entire hotel. Apparently, it's where he always stayed when he visited. He was lucky to get the room at such short notice. Possibly the fact it cost so much meant it often stayed empty.

Daisy had a connecting room. Hers was pretty darn impressive, too. It had a view of Avenue Montaigne, a marble bathroom, an essential oil capsule diffuser in the shower. And on her bed, a bottle of Champagne in an ice

CHAPTER 11 - DAISY

bucket, some French pastries, and a note that read, *Enjoy your adventure, Daisy Grove. x*

Daisy put down her luggage, a big grin on her face. She opened up her bag and took out her prize possession: the Fairy Godmother pillowcase.

"Just one thing this room is missing," she said, putting the pillowcase over the puffiest pillow on the bed. "There! That's better."

She looked around, wondering what to do next. Eat a croissant, pop open the fizz, or knock on the adjoining door and wait for her boss to ravish her senseless...Maybe she could somehow manage all three things at once.

Just as she was pondering this, the phone on her bedside table rang. *Yeep!* She almost jumped out of her skin. She scurried over to pick it up and was surprised to hear Montague on the other end.

"Fifteen minutes until our boat tour starts, little mouse."

"Boat tour? Fifteen minutes?"

Daisy really should have checked the schedule during that long flight. She hadn't gotten the hang of this PA job very well yet. She guessed she'd been a bit distracted these last few days...

"We're going on a private boat tour of the Seine," Montague told her. "Remember? The party boat?"

Of course. The party boat. One of the activities planned for the DDlg trip to Paris was a party boat along the Seine. A disco for the Littles, and a poker area for the Daddies. She'd forgotten they were supposed to be testing out the boat route.

"Oh yes," she said, looking at the treats on her bed, trying not to sound disappointed. "So...do we have fifteen minutes until we go, or do we have to leave—"

"We have to leave now," he told her. "But don't you dare leave the Champagne and pastries behind."

Daisy bit her lip, tears filling her eyes. Why did she keep getting so darned emotional? "Okay," she said. "I won't, boss."

She picked up the bottle and the pastries and stuffed them into her handbag. As she did so, her cellphone buzzed. She rifled through her bag for it, feeling faintly irritated. Whoever it was messaging her, they had better leave her alone after this. She didn't need the real world interrupting her while she was here, thank you very much.

Oh, great.

It was Raymond again.

A short message this time.

When am I gonna get that second chance, baby?

She punched in a reply immediately.

Please leave me alone, Raymond. I'm sorry to hurt you, but it's over.

She hit send before she had time to back out. She had never really stood up to him before—had never felt able to. But this was a time for new beginnings. You couldn't have an adventure without being a little brave.

Everything had been perfect. The boat tour. The Champagne. The flakiest croissants in the history of croissants.

But there was more. The sunset. The handbag Montague bought her because hers was full of croissant crumbs. A handbag that just so happened to be a preloved Louis Vuitton from the Takashi Murakami *multicolore* collection. Bright, candy-colored monograms that were somehow sophisticated and youthful at the same time.

And then there was the Michelin-star meal. White asparagus. Tomato sea bass. Peaches and cheese, which sounded kinda out there, but it really freaking worked.

And then there was *him*. The man she called Daddy. The man she called boss. The man she called sir when he was spanking her bare bottom. The man she hoped would spank her bare bottom again very, very soon.

Montague was the perfect gentleman all evening. He was the ideal travel companion too. A tour guide and a teacher. A best friend and a...boyfriend.

Okay, okay, he wasn't actually her boyfriend.

But he already felt like more of a boyfriend than Raymond had ever been.

CHAPTER 11 - DAISY

It was crazy that she was here in Paris, somewhere that Raymond had talked about so often. He often talked about the two of them moving there together. Just as soon as his work got picked up by a major publisher, he'd told her, they'd get a little apartment on the Seine. They'd drink red wine and smoke cigarettes and live like F. Scott Fitzgerald and his wife, Zelda. Knowing what had happened to the Fitzgeralds, Daisy had always seen that as something of a threat.

They *had* booked a honeymoon in Paris, though. It had been Daisy's idea because she knew that Raymond never would get his work picked up by a major publisher, and she had been impatient to visit the French capital. In fact, the honeymoon in Paris had been the one thing about her marriage that she'd looked forward to: The city of love. She knew that going with Raymond would have spoiled it, though.

Being here with Montague was a lesson in how to be looked after. He opened doors for her. He pointed out interesting things to her. He helped her to pick meals that he thought she'd enjoy. He was so much better than a boyfriend. He was a *man*friend. Mature. Thoughtful. Protective. After all, he was a Daddy.

And unfortunately, her Daddy had kissed her on the cheek ten minutes ago and then retired to his room.

Now, here she was, standing in her beautiful hotel room, all alone. There was nothing but a locked door between them, but she may as well have been on the other side of the planet.

"Oh, Daddy," she whispered. "You don't need to be so polite. Just walk in here and rip my clothes off."

Unfortunately, her desperate whisper did not make Montague magically materialize, so she ran herself a bath, enjoying the delightful Guerlain toiletries, and then slipped under the covers, naked. It was such a luxury to be able to sleep without her clothes—and shoes—on. And there wasn't a creepy laughing man to be heard anywhere. She began to drift off into a sweet and dreamy sleep, full of visions of all the things she might encounter the following day at Disneyland with her Daddy...

But only minutes later, her cellphone buzzed.

Shoot. She should have switched that thing off. She didn't need any more interruptions from Raymond.

When she checked the screen, though, she was surprised to see that the message was from Montague.

Are you up? I need you.

She started to write a message back, then she deleted it. He was only through the other side of the wall. This was silly. She groped for her glasses then got out of bed and slipped on a bathrobe. She grabbed her work notepad, then knocked on the adjoining door.

She heard his footsteps padding over to the door, heard the lock being turned, and then saw him there, in a tight white t-shirt and snug blue boxers. She'd only ever seen him in a suit before, and the sight did something to her. Something very pleasant.

It was hard to say what she liked best about him. The bulge of his biceps. The hardness of his pecs beneath the t-shirt. The flatness of his belly. The curve of his cock. The thickness of his thighs...

"What is it, sir?" she asked, pencil poised, her eyes darting around the suite, which was so posh it was like being on a movie set. Fresh flowers, golden ornaments, several balconies. "Need to dictate something to me?"

"I can't sleep." He sighed, walking to the bedroom. She saw a small bottle on the bed and recognized it as a miniature Scotch from the minibar. He sat on the edge of the mattress and rubbed his chin. His stubble made a slightly scratchy noise, which for some reason turned Daisy on.

"I'm sorry to hear that, sir," said Daisy. "It can be hard to sleep in a new place. And you probably have a lot of work on your mind—"

"It would have been my father's birthday today," he interjected. "I think I need you to help me with that trick. Five minutes of fun."

Daisy felt a pang of guilt. Here she was, getting turned on thinking naughty thoughts about her Daddy, and he was grieving for his dead father. A father who had been cruel to him, but a father nonetheless.

"What did you have in mind?" she asked. "How about a pillow fight?

Ooh! Or we could play Bucking Bronco on your big bed—"

He put his finger to his lips. "Daisy," he said, "my sweet girl. I just had a perfect evening with you, but I don't want to rush things. This isn't some sordid affair for me. I have never had a relationship with anyone at work before. And it's been a long time since I fucked anyone at all, in all honesty." He paused. "I have a tendency to jump right into things. I'm an impatient man, in case you hadn't noticed. But with you...I want to do things differently."

Daisy shivered at his words. She felt the same way, only kinda the opposite. She had a tendency to wait around for things forever. But with him, she wanted to jump in headfirst.

"I'm most likely not the man for you," Montague continued. "I'm too old for you. I'm addicted to work. I'm grumpy as hell. And I hate marriage and everything it stands for. But..."

"But what, sir?" asked Daisy, her voice suddenly hoarse.

Montague reached out for her. He took her hands in his, then pulled her close to him. "I can't get you out of my head, little mouse."

Daisy's entire body was trembling. "What is it you're thinking about, sir?"

"I don't want to offend you."

"Try me," she said quietly.

Montague ran his tongue across his lips. "I can't stop thinking about tying your wrists to this headboard with my belt and then fucking your mouth until I come."

Daisy felt moisture from her pussy trickle down the inside of her thigh. "If it'll help you sleep, sir," she said, "then I guess we'd better do it. Five minutes of fun, right?"

CHAPTER 12 - MONTAGUE

Montague couldn't believe how submissive Daisy was. How happy she was to go along with even his most demanding propositions. He really had hit the jackpot when he met her. The moment he had instructed her to take off her bathrobe, she had complied, letting it fall into a heap on the floor. Then, at his request, she had fondled her breasts for him.

God damn, she was beautiful. Her breasts were small, but perfectly formed. Her pale pink nipples invited his lips, his tongue, his teeth to get to know them better. That beautiful V-shape nestled at the top of her legs was every bit as wonderful as he'd remembered. The soft dark hair curling at the top. No doubt her real hair color beneath the bleach. He loved seeing the real her. The her that she'd never felt the need to change for the outside world. The her that only the truly privileged got to see.

"Before we do this," he told her, "I have one condition."

"Yes, sir?"

Good girl. She'd remembered he liked to be called sir when they were engaging in a scene. And this was most definitely going to be a scene.

"I want you to leave your glasses on," he told her.

Daisy stopped touching her breasts and blinked at him from behind her yellow spectacles.

She'd never believe it–especially since she was bullied for wearing them as a child–but she looked so damn sexy with them on.

"Really?" she asked. "Aren't they a bit...off-putting?"

"Sweetheart," he said, "they've been turning me on from day one. You look like Velma from *Scooby Doo*. One of my childhood crushes."

"My glasses are nothing like hers," Daisy said, giggling.

"Same effect," he told her. "Studious, but fun. Outrageously flirtatious in an extremely sneaky way."

"Is that what I am?" Daisy asked. "Outrageously flirtatious in an extremely sneaky way?"

"You most definitely are," Montague replied. "You're a Little, after all. Littles are some of the sneakiest people on the planet."

He began to touch her now, running his palms up and down her body, stroking her soft skin, wondering what the hell someone as perfect as her was doing with an old curmudgeon like him.

"Sounds quite naughty of me," Daisy said, biting her lip.

"You see, there you go again," he said. "Being sneaky." He tutted disapprovingly as he pushed a finger into her mouth, and she bit down on it. "Uh oh," he said. "I'd better restrain you before there's any more of this naughty behavior. Don't forget that Daddy can change his mind about doing sexy things any time he wants and give you a good spanking instead."

He lifted her up onto the bed then lay her on her back, lifting her arms above her head. He'd always thought the elegant wooden headboard on this King-sized bed would be perfect for restraining someone, but he'd never had anyone with him to try it out. Now, he had the most tempting woman in the world: Daisy Grove. A woman named after flowers and trees. A woman sprouted from the earth just for him.

He took his leather belt off the back of a chair and tied it securely around Daisy's wrists. Tight, but not so tight it would hurt her if she wriggled.

"Don't forget your safeword," he warned her.

"Bibbity-bobbity-boo," she said.

"Bless you," he joked. He finished securing the belt to the headboard and then said: "If you can't speak because my cock is in your mouth, then just knock on wood. Okay?"

Daisy just about managed to knock on the headboard and grinned. "Will that bring me good luck?"

"It sure brought me good luck," Montague replied. It was strange—he wasn't used to joking around like this. He'd always thought that starting up a scene like this would be one-hundred-percent serious. All rules and gravitas.

CHAPTER 12 - MONTAGUE

But Daisy made everything fun. And reminded him what it was that he liked about all this stuff in the first place. BDSM was meant to be an escape from the seriousness of his everyday life. It was meant to be *enjoyable*.

"Actually, I think it's a little bit naughty of *you*, sir, to be the one who gets to orgasm first," Daisy said. "After all, you were about to make me climax back at the office. We still have unfinished business in that regard, don't we?" She looked up at him, fluttering her lashes.

"Just you wait until tomorrow," he told her. "I have something in mind that's gonna have you coming over and over again."

Daisy looked puzzled. "At Disneyland?"

"Mm-hmm," Montague replied. "Ever heard of love eggs, Daisy? I have a pair in my luggage with your name on them."

Daisy blushed. "Ooh. Daisy eggs."

"First thing's first, though," said Montague, taking off his t-shirt. He could feel her eyes boring into his skin, checking out every line on his finely-chiseled body. Thankfully, with all the workouts he did at his home gym, he wasn't self-conscious in that regard. He might have been a few years older than her, but he was in good shape. And he was going to need to be to keep up with this Little one. He could sense it.

"Daddy's been thinking dirty thoughts about you for far too long now," he said, looking down at her prone form that was stretched out naked and immobile for him. He pulled down his pants, aware that he already had a semi. "I need to let off a little steam before tomorrow. Tomorrow's your day, after all. I'm gonna need complete focus."

Daisy nodded solemnly, but he could see how excited she was. Her gaze traveled down to his cock, and he grabbed hold of it, showing her how thick and hard he was capable of getting it.

I might be older than you, babygirl, but I've got the energy of ten men when you're around...

He stroked his shaft a couple times, and his cock responded perfectly. Then, he climbed onto the bed on all fours, bending down to kiss Daisy on the lips, his cock dipping down and brushing against her inner thigh. He felt her

107

shudder and he pressed his cock down harder, teasing her.

Holy fuck, he wanted to slide his dick inside of her right now. He wanted to fuck his babygirl senseless, to claim her not just for now, but forever.

But he could wait. She was worth it.

Tomorrow, he would hand her the contract he'd drawn up. Make everything official. Tonight, he would simply squirt his cum down her throat. It hadn't been part of his plan, but he'd gotten down tonight thinking about his father. He'd had a wonderful evening up until the point he'd said goodnight to Daisy and come back to his own room. On his own, he'd had time to brood. Now, he wanted to undo that brooding.

And besides, he deserved this, didn't he? He'd been all work and no play for so long.

And Daisy seemed very, very into the idea. She was squirming on his bedsheets already, lifting up her hips, trying to coax his dick into her juicy little pussy.

"Not yet, babygirl," he told her. "Don't be impatient." He cupped her breasts, massaging them as he kissed her sweet lips, feeling his cock grow harder still, blooming and straining at the tip.

He put a couple pillows under her head, to get her at just the right angle. Then, he stroked his cock some more and it was a challenge not to come immediately. It felt so much better than when he touched himself alone. She was the full package. The sight, the sound, the smell, the touch...the taste.. Damn, he couldn't wait to taste every inch of her. But right now, she had a job to do.

"Open your mouth for me," he ordered her. "I need to feel that pretty little throat of yours."

Daisy opened her mouth obediently, and he didn't waste any time in sliding his dick right in there. She felt just as he'd hoped. Wet, warm, snug. He rubbed his cock up and down on her tongue, loving how still she was staying for him. He'd never thought about having a sex slave or anything as extreme as that, but right now, with Daisy, the idea was growing on him. It drove him wild to think about her chained up in his Miami compound, her mouth or her anus clamped open while he did whatever the hell he wanted with her.

He'd never hurt her, obviously. He'd never do anything that she didn't want to do. But what he liked about Daisy was it felt like he'd finally met his match. The girl who seemed to be his perfect opposite. Light where he was dark. Open where he was closed. Submissive where he was dominant. The girl who radiated sunshine, even when his cock was six inches down her throat.

He thrust inside her harder now, enjoying the grunts she made as he forced her lips farther open. He stole glances at her hands every now and then, making sure she was free to knock on the headboard if she wanted to. She *was* free, of course, but there was no way she was about to knock in a million years.

It was time to allow himself the release he'd been so ardently craving.

The release that his body needed so very fucking bad.

The release he'd been waiting for, for days, months, years.

He felt it well up inside him like a storm, then, when the storm was at its most powerful, he felt everything crackle, and his semen rained down the back of her throat, a burst cloud.

Relief.

She felt like heaven. Swallowing him up like that. Drinking away all that pent-up energy–energy that was no longer serving him. She had taken it away from him and made the storm into sunshine.

His amazing Little girl.

He slid out of her mouth and looked down at her. Her eyes were lazy and glazed over, as though *she* had just climaxed too. But that was impossible, wasn't it?

"Babygirl," he whispered. "That was incredible."

She nodded, unable to get any words out.

He knew how intense the experience must have been for her, and he undid the leather straps then he held her close to him, kissing her mouth, her neck, her chest. They weren't *sex* kisses anymore. They were something deeper than that. Kisses of connection. Kisses of promise.

"I owe you...everything," he told her, overcome with gratitude to the universe for allowing her to walk into his life. "Before I met you, my lovely flower, I had forgotten how to feel joy. I was stuck under a constant raincloud. You know, I couldn't even remember what it felt like to be a kid anymore? But now, being with you, watching you live in the moment...it's sublime." He smiled, holding his chest against hers, letting his heart speak to her. "You know, I remembered my favorite candy the other day, from when I was a kid. Dubble Bubble. The color of your eyes and your glasses reminded me of them. Being with you is like eating Dubble Bubble. Pure delight." He looked deep into her eyes.

"Daddy," she moaned, finally able to speak. "Daddy, I'm yours."

"You *are*, sweet babygirl," he told her. "And tomorrow, I'll prove that to you."

She smiled, looking up at him. "What's tomorrow?"

"Tomorrow," he said, pressing the tip of her nose, "is a very important day for us. Tomorrow is...the day we get to meet Mickey Mouse."

Daisy laughed. "I thought you were going to say something more profound than that."

"I was," Montague said. "But you know what? I'm gonna save the surprise for tomorrow."

"Aww, no fair," Daisy humphed.

"And you, Little one, need to get some sleep now. I want you fresh in the morning."

Daisy yawned. "Yes, Daddy."

"Good girl. I'll see you tomorrow then." He kissed her on the lips, then lifted her off the bed and patted her bottom.

"Um." She was hesitating, though he wasn't sure why. "Am I...sleeping in *my* room then?"

"Darling, if you stay in my room, I won't get an ounce of sleep," Montague said. He raised an eyebrow. "And nor will you."

Daisy blushed and bit her lip. "Okay, Daddy. Sweet dreams."

With that, she scampered off, leaving him to immediately regret his decision.

Fuck. He was so out of practice at this. He should have probably provided aftercare for her for longer. He should have definitely invited her to sleep in bed with him.

It was just...

He hadn't been lying about the sleep thing. It had been so long since he'd shared a bed with someone. The last person he'd shared a mattress with had been Olga, actually, and that was far from pleasant. With someone as perfect as Daisy beside him, tempting him...he was bound to get carried away. And staying up all night would undoubtedly ruin their plans for an early breakfast. Which, in turn, would ruin everything he had planned after that.

And he really, really didn't want to spoil Daisy's day tomorrow.

CHAPTER 13 - DAISY

Five in the morning. Normally a time that no human should ever have to be awake. It was way too late to still be up, and way too early to not be sleeping.

And yet.

Daisy hadn't managed to sleep a wink.

Not. A. Freaking. Wink.

Her heart had been cantering around her chest with excitement.

She had been replaying that scene with Montague over and over and over. The feeling of the leather restraints around her wrists. The noise he made, deep and throaty, when he came. The salty taste of him. The way he kissed her afterward.

Her ex, Raymond, had never dominated her. Not like that, anyway. He'd dominated her in nasty ways. Bullying, really. She'd probably put up with it so long because of her submissive tendencies. But she never got anything *sexual* out of it. In fact, he was useless at that kind of domination. She asked him once if he'd be open to taking control in the bedroom. He'd slapped her face and called her a "dirty bitch" while fucking her. Another time he'd tried to throttle her. And then there was that other time. That time when he was very, very drunk and he stopped having sex with her and decided to pee all over her instead.

She wasn't into the pee especially, but she wasn't into *any* of those things. Not with him, at any rate. Not when they seemed to be performed out of malice or ineptitude. She had this feeling that if Montague put *his* hands around her neck, he'd find a way to make it sexy. He could even slap her face in a way she enjoyed if it was part of a scene. As for the peeing...not so much, probably, but then who knew? It felt as though the whole world had opened up before her.

LUCKY MOON

When she'd come back to her room last night, at first she'd been a little disappointed. She'd wanted to spend the night curled up next to her Daddy. But she had appreciated his reasoning for sending her back to her room. And she knew that it was a difficult night for him, being his father's birthday and everything. Maybe he needed some alone time. She respected that. Raymond had never, ever wanted alone time.

The problem was, she'd been so freaking turned on last night. Montague hadn't touched her private parts all night, but she'd come back to her room feeling like they were on fire. Aching to be touched, licked, fucked. Naturally, she'd touched herself. More than once. In fact, she'd kind of been touching herself all night long. On the bed. On the couch. In the bath. She had an unquenchable thirst within her–a thirst which could only be sated with him.

At five in the morning, she felt like she might just burst with excitement. Because there was only one hour left until breakfast time. Strangely, she hadn't even thought about Disneyland that much. She was only thinking about him. Montague, Montague, Montague. She couldn't wait to breakfast with him. To wear Daisy eggs with him. To *everything* with him.

Giving up on sleep, she hopped out of bed and peeped outside at the amazing view. Even though it was still so early, there were still people walking around. Paris was unlike any other place she'd ever been. Everything had been crafted with such thought. Such attention to detail. The curve of the lampposts. The glass canopies over doors. The gold-tipped fences. The whole city was the perfect mix of art and history. And it was so alive, too. Buzzing with people and ideas.

It was summertime, which meant that the sun was already up. Daisy opened up the balcony door and perched on the little bistro-style seat. In the natural light, she could make out slight marks on her wrists that reminded her of last night. She smiled as she replayed the scene for the millionth time.

The weight of his body pressing down on her. His cock stretching her lips wide. His grunts and groans of desire.

Come on, Daisy. Snap out of it. You'll turn into a sex zombie.

She focused on the feeling of the fresh air on her face. The sound of the

114

trees on Avenue Montaigne, their leaves rustling in the breeze.

She felt her breathing slow, her head droop toward her chest.

And then she heard a knock.

Startling, she realized that she had fallen asleep. She checked the clock in her room. Six o'clock. Thank goodness! She hadn't missed anything. In fact, the hour of sleep had rejuvenated her. A power nap.

The knock sounded at her door again and she yawned as she walked over to it. Okay, she wasn't *completely* rejuvenated, but it's nothing a few cups of coffee wouldn't sort out. Plus, she was certain to wake up the moment that she saw Montag—

"Bonjour, madame," said a friendly-looking woman wearing red lipstick standing in the hall. She was holding a silver tray with a silver dome on it. Beside the dome was a small yellow box with a white envelope beside it.

"I don't think that's for me," Daisy said. "I have plans for breakfast this morning."

"The gentleman in the adjoining room asked us to send this to you," she said in a strong French accent. "Shall I bring it in?"

"Sure."

Daisy watched, puzzled, as the maid left her tray on the table by the window, then bid her "au revoir" and left the room.

What was Montague up to now? He was always surprising her.

She opened up the dome and stared, confused, at the Croque Madame beneath. The egg yolk stared up at her, trying to tell her something.

"I don't understand..." she said to the egg. "Montague said he'd knock on my door and take me down to breakfast...Is he planning on breakfast in bed?"

She looked at the yellow box on the tray...and then it hit her.

Oh my goodness. The love eggs.

He had sent them to her room so that she could wear them down to breakfast. But wait. She had her breakfast here. Maybe he thought she'd need some time to get used to them in private, so he'd sent her breakfast in bed.

She grabbed the envelope with a smile on her face, waiting to see what his instructions were. Inside the envelope, she found the company credit card and a short message.

Little mouse, it said. *Urgent business called me back to Miami. Will explain when you get back. Say hi to Mickey for me. If he asks you to be his PA, tell him he can't have you. You're mine.*

She read the note three more times, each time slower than the last, as if trying to decode a foreign language. What on earth was he talking about? Was this a joke? Urgent business called him back to Miami? In the middle of the night?

And did he honestly expect her to wear the Daisy eggs without him here? Quickly, she opened the yellow box, ready to toss them over the side of the balcony in anger.

But there weren't any love eggs in there. There was a single piece of candy. A yellow and blue wrapper, with two words in capital letters: "DUBBLE BUBBLE."

Oh no.

This was a goodbye.

Now, it dawned on her. She'd moved too fast. She should have taken things *so* much slower. He'd gotten what he wanted and left.

Maybe she shouldn't have allowed things to develop at all. A PA and her boss. It wasn't right. It was maybe even illegal.

God. What if he'd hated the way she'd sucked his cock? It was difficult to get the right angle, being strapped down like that. What if he'd thought that was the best she could manage?

Probably he didn't like her body. Her breasts were on the small side. Her nipples were so pale you could hardly see them. Her frame was slim, but her belly still stuck out a bit. Was that normal? And what about her cellulite? It's not like she had much, but there were definite dimples there.

Urgh.

She looked at the egg on her Croque Madame accusingly. "Stop looking at me like that. I messed up. I know I did."

Her tummy rumbled in spite of her annoyance.

"Fine. But just so you know, I'm not happy about this."

CHAPTER 13 - DAISY

She picked up the knife and fork and cut a chunk out of the Croque Madame and the egg yolk oozed down onto the plate perfectly. But...

Darn it. She couldn't eat. It felt wrong.

Instead, she unwrapped the Dubble Bubble candy, put it in her mouth, and chewed angrily. She blew a bubble even *more* angrily. Immediately, the bubble burst.

Daisy was an expert on Cinderella castles around the world. She'd always loved the classic, elegant design of the castle at Disney World, Florida, and it would no doubt remain her favorite. But the castle at Disneyland Paris had its plus points, for sure. Bright and colorful, inspired by the chateaux of the Loire Valley, including elements of all the Disney castles to date, and with fun little touches. For instance, one of the turrets had snail shells stuck all over it as a nod to French *escargots*. And there was also an animatronic dragon under the castle, which was pretty freaking cool. Technically, of course, it was a Sleeping Beauty castle. But that didn't matter to Daisy. A castle at Disney would always be a Cinderella castle in her eyes.

As she roamed around Disneyland, wearing a *Cinderella* t-shirt and tiara from the gift shop, eating a chocolate-dipped Mickey-shaped meringue–all bought using the company credit card, of course–Daisy barely looked at the castle. She barely looked at anything. Everywhere she went, all she saw was betrayal. It hurt her, actually, to have to be here. To have to associate one of her most beloved places on earth with *him*. Yet another man who had let her down.

She'd been such an idiot to dive right into another relationship. She was on the rebound. She was meant to be getting married two and a half weeks ago, for Pete's sake. To a cruel, manipulative man who didn't treat her right.

Huh. Clearly, she had a type.

She bit into the Mickey meringue, which was going gooey in the sticky heat. She wondered what to do with her life now.

Could she really go back to working at Daddies Inc. after this? She was still on her probation. She could quit right now if she wanted to, without even bothering with a notice period. No point going back to that lousy trailer, anyhow.

But the company credit card wouldn't be hers to use, and she had no cash. She could call her friends and ask them to lend her a few hundred dollars to start her off…They wouldn't, though. Not to do something as crazy as starting a new life in Paris. Besides, she didn't really want it. France was a beautiful country with a beautiful language and beautiful people, but it wasn't home. Corn dogs, and the Grand Canyon, and baseball, and country music, and fruit Roll-Ups were home. Her friends were home.

Her eyes pricked with tears.

She should never have left Peach and Kiera to go to Miami. She should never have tried to have an adventure on her own.

She let out a long sigh and took her cell phone out her pocket. She opened up the group chat she used to talk to her friends and wrote them a message.

Guys, I'm sorry about running away. You were right. I was dumb to move to Miami. I miss you both so much. I lied about the company I'm working for. I work for a man called Montague Manners. He's a Daddy Dom and he kind of used me. I'm in Paris at the moment, but will explain everything soon. I love you. I'm coming home. x

The second she finished her message, she felt a tap on her shoulder. A man's voice spoke close to her ear.

"Found you."

Montague?

She turned, her pulse racing, and when she saw who it was, her heart raced faster still. "Raymond?"

"Daisy-doo," he replied, taking her cellphone out of her hand.

"Give that back!" she cried.

He didn't. He pocketed it.

He was standing there in the exact same outfit he'd been wearing the day she left him. The very same suit he'd worn at the altar. The only thing that was different was that now he sported a thick beard, red-rimmed eyes, and he was wearing a navy blue baseball cap. The cap said "I'M NOT A SNOB–I'M JUST BETTER THAN YOU" on it. What had she been thinking to stay with someone like that for so long?

"What are you doing here?" she asked, backing away. "What's going on?" Her eyes flitted left and right, looking for a park security guard. Someone who could help her if things got heavy. Right now, she couldn't see anyone except the chipmunks: Alvin, Simon, and Theodore. Could they help her in a pinch?

"It's a good thing you've been keeping your Find My Friends app on," he told her. "And if you ask me, it's a sign."

Daisy swallowed. "A sign?"

Raymond stepped toward her. "You're playing hide-and-seek, Daisy-doo."

Daisy held what remained of her meringue up defensively, as though using it as a shield. "No, I'm not."

"You *wanted* me to find you."

Daisy shook her head adamantly. "No. I want to be alone. Please give me back my phone and leave me alone, Raymond."

Raymond took the meringue from her and bit into it.

She noticed his white teeth as he did so. One of the things about him that she'd first noticed, that had first attracted her to him. Perfectly straight, white teeth. Now, she saw those teeth as nothing but weapons. Another tool at his disposal for hurting her. Well, at least if he bit her, she could bite back.

"You obviously came out here because you still have feelings for me," he said. "Your subconscious mind is out here looking for a future with me."

"No," said Daisy. "It's not."

Raymond smiled. It wasn't a warm smile. It was a cold, scary smile. A smile that froze her to the spot.

"Daisy," he said. "I know you better than you know yourself. And trust me when I tell you that you've gone a little off-the-rails lately. Running around all over the place. Acting childish. Putting yourself in dangerous situations—"

"There's nothing dangerous about Disneyland. It's one of the safest places on earth—"

"Maybe not, but that trailer park is pretty dangerous, don't you think?"

Daisy closed her eyes, trying to block out Raymond's words. Had he really followed her to the trailer park too? She imagined for a moment that *he* was the laughing man. The man who had been tormenting her nights for way too long now. But of course that hadn't been him. Just some other creepy man in a world of creepy men.

"Are you stalking me, Raymond?" she asked quietly. If he was, did that mean he knew about Montague? About everything?

Raymond reached out for her, holding her shoulders with a grip so forceful it would likely leave bruises. "Daisy, my Daisy, I'm *protecting* you. I never went to Miami, as it happened. I was just watching your whereabouts on the app. I've been in Paris this whole time." He smiled. "On our honeymoon."

Daisy swallowed. "Our honeymoon was only meant to be for two weeks."

"Yeah, well I was at the airport, about to fly back to Connecticut when guess what? I saw my little Daisy-doo on her way out to meet me."

"I wasn't coming here for you. I didn't even know you were here. I thought you'd have got a refund for the honeymoon, seeing as how we never got married."

Raymond spread his arms wide. "I never gave up on you, Daisy. On us. I've been watching and waiting for the big sign. And now here it is. And here I am."

"This isn't a sign," Daisy said. "This is a work thing. I'm here for work."

Raymond laughed. "You really have gone completely cuckoo, eh? Lucky for you, I accept you for who you are, ugly yellow glasses and all. I promise to love you in sickness and in health, forever and ever." He paused. "As long as we both shall live."

"I want to go now, Raymond," Daisy said. "I want my phone."

"What you want," Raymond told her, "is to find true happiness. And it just so happens that I have it all planned out."

"You have *what* planned out?"

"The wedding of your dreams," Raymond said. "I get it now. The reason you walked away before. It wasn't big enough. Special enough. Lucky for you, the moment I saw where you were headed I got us a booking. We're going to get married *today*, Daisy. Isn't that amazing? I found a slot for us the Davy Crockett Ranch. You like Davy Crockett, right?"

"No," Daisy protested. "I don't want to do that."

"Oh, but you do," said Raymond, an air of menace in his voice. "You really, really do."

CHAPTER 14 - MONTAGUE

———

This airplane was suffocating. Montague paced up and down the tiny cabin, much to the annoyance of the other business class members.

It was torture not being able to call her.

It was torture to have left her so abruptly.

It was torture not to be there with her now.

He imagined them both at Disney World, eating crepes and potato *gratin*, going on ride after ride after ride. He was meant to be showing her the contract around now. He had it all planned out. They were going to sign the contract at Sleeping Beauty's castle. And then he'd booked a surprise for her. A private tour run by the Fairy Godmother from *Cinderella*, followed by a champagne dinner in the *Auberge de Cendrillon*, a Cinderella-themed medieval banqueting hall. He had plans to make Daisy feel like a real princess for the day. A princess who happened to be wearing love eggs.

And then, of course, there was tonight. He'd planned a table at the Moulin Rouge, stopping off at the most exclusive stores the Erotic District of Paris had to offer. And then back to the hotel, to let his princess become his queen...

Instead, he was here. Stuck in a tin can, flying over an endless expanse of ocean, every passing second taking him farther and farther away from her.

"I don't have time for this," he muttered, still pacing.

Unfortunately, the reason for having to abandon Daisy was too pressing to ignore.

Last night, he'd received an email from his lawyer. Things with Olga had escalated. She didn't *just* want his compound anymore. Oh, no. Why stop there? Now, she wanted everything. Everything except the houseboat.

And that list of everything included:

The vineyard.

The cabin at Lake Tahoe.

The private jet timeshare.

The stocks in Warren Buffet's company, Berkshire Hathaway.

The Aston Martin. The Ferrari. And of course, his beloved Bentley.

Oh, and his dead father's house.

The only thing she didn't want was the houseboat. Which proved how much of a heathen she was, because that houseboat was the fucking bomb.

Olga had always had bad taste, though. Three months into her relationship, she used his platinum card to buy *gold pills*. And what did the gold pills do? Make her rich? Make her look ten years younger? Turn her into a good person? Nope. They did not. They made her literally shit glitter. Gold fucking excrement. It really summed up that woman.

Montague had his reasons for getting together with Olga in the first place. She was a Russian beauty, in a harsh kind of a way. And she was a performance artist, which Montague had found intriguing for all of five minutes. The performance she'd been working on when they'd met was called 'Little Olga.' For the show, she'd sat in a gallery surrounded by oversized furniture, wearing a romper suit, and listening to lullabies. He had been a sucker to think there was truth behind the performance. Olga wasn't a Little in real life. She was more like...a vampire.

It didn't take long before Montague started to find her performances disturbing, to say the least. Bloodletting on stage. Hanging upside-down until she fainted. Throwing live cats at a pane of glass.

He'd already broken things off with her by the time the cat thing happened. Or at least, he'd tried to. The moment the words had escaped from his mouth, she'd told him she was pregnant.

And the baby was his.

The thing about Montague was that he was an honorable man. His father hadn't been one—he'd had various mistresses while he was married to Montague's mother. He'd lied and let Montague's mother down over and over again. He never hit her, but he didn't have to. His words and actions hurt her so deeply that her pain couldn't have been any greater. Eventually, she'd left him. But by then it was too late. She was scarred for life. Never trusted anyone ever again. Never allowed herself to feel joy. Never let herself be loved.

Montague swore he didn't want to turn out like his father. He wasn't a womanizer. He valued his partners and stuck by them through thick and thin. So he did the right thing. He offered to marry Olga, to bring up the child they were having together, and to try—as well as he could—to make his family happy.

The day after their wedding, Olga told Montague that she wasn't actually pregnant. The pregnancy had been yet another performance, she had informed him. Then she went out to throw some cats at some glass.

So, after a six-million-dollar wedding and a hell of a lot of stress, Montague told Olga the marriage was over before it had begun. They slept in separate beds for a week, until Montague kicked Olga out of his home for good.

He screwed his eyes tight shut, trying to block out the painful memory. His father had been alive back then and had found the whole thing hilarious.

"You dumb fuck," he'd said, wiping the tears of laughter from his eyes. "She had you good, eh? Always knew you were a gullible halfwit, but that is something else."

Now, his dad was dead and Olga wanted to take his old home. The home Montague grew up in. And it didn't matter how shitty a father Hubert Manners had been. Montague deserved that house. It was his family fucking home. He'd earned it.

This was only part of the reason that Montague was rushing back to the States, though. Because on top of everything else, Olga wanted Daddies Inc. She wanted all of his shares in the company. And that could *never* happen. She'd have voting power in the company. She'd run the whole place into the ground, probably as part of some fucked-up performance piece. If Daddies Inc. fell apart, it would let down so many people, Daisy included.

"I can't let that happen," he muttered.

"Are you okay, son?" asked a man sitting in the seat nearest his. "You've been pacing up and down for over an hour."

Montague rubbed his face, trying to snap himself out of his mood. "Got a lot on my mind," he muttered, returning to his seat.

"Want to talk about it?" the man asked. He put down his magazine and removed his glasses. His forehead was lined. Way more lined than Montague's. And he was mostly bald, too. Looked around sixty-three. His dad's age when he'd...expired. How had this man's heart managed to keep beating when his dad's had not? What was his secret?

Montague shook his head. "I prefer not to talk about my feelings."

And I prefer not to talk to strangers, as it happens.

The man winked. "I think if I didn't talk about my feelings, I'd get hella grumpy."

Montague snorted, but he didn't laugh. He never laughed, just like he never cried, and he never talked to goddamn strangers if he could help it.

"Well, if you change your mind..." the man said.

Montague didn't have time for this. He needed to think. To formulate a plan to kick Olga out of his life for good. "Not gonna happen," he said. "And believe me, that's best for both of us. I'd be chewing your ear off the whole way back to Miami."

The man smiled. "Betcha it's simpler than you think," he said. "Just start with what makes you angriest. Then what makes you saddest. And end with what makes you happiest."

Montague looked at him with interest. "You know a lot about this, huh?"

He laughed. "Well, this has been my job for forty years. You don't get to fly business class after all that time unless you turned out to be good at what you did."

In spite of himself, Montague almost smiled. He felt a tiny flicker at the corner of his lips. But it felt good all the same.

He really *didn't* have time for this, but there was something oddly appealing about the idea of offloading all his shit onto a complete stranger. Maybe strangers *did* have their uses. Besides, Daisy had been a stranger once. She wasn't one anymore. Far from it. Maybe strangers were worth the time.

"All right," he said. "I'll bite."

CHAPTER 14 - MONTAGUE

He couldn't believe he was about to get a free therapy session on an airplane from a guy he just met. Plus, just as the man had said, he *had* to be good at what he did to be flying business class. Montague respected that.

"What makes me angriest..." he said. "That's easy. The answer is Olga. She's my soon-to-be *ex*-wife. Just as soon as she agrees to the fuckin—I mean *damn*—no wait, is that any better?"

"Don't worry about cursing around me, son," said the man. "Just speak from the heart."

"As soon as she agrees to the damn divorce," said Montague, grateful for not having to self-censor.

"What about makes you saddest?"

Montague closed his eyes and took a deep breath. "My father."

"Were you close?"

He shook his head. "We were just about as far apart as it's possible for two beings to be. And now he's dead, and I don't know how to feel."

"Interesting," said the man.

"It is?" Montague blinked at him, confused.

"When you spoke about your wife, you looked totally detached. But when you spoke about your father, you clenched your fists and tightened your jaw. I have a feeling that what you're angriest about, deep down, is your relationship with *him*."

Montague shook his head. "I don't want to waste energy on being angry with that bully. Besides, he was my father. There's some kind of bond there, no matter how hard you try not to—"

"It's okay to feel two things at once," said the man. "It's okay to feel angry and sad at the same time. And it's okay to let yourself experience both of those emotions at their deepest level."

Montague grimaced. "I don't really *do* emotions. Except grumpy."

The man shrugged. "Try it. Spend five minutes now, feeling as angry and sad as you like."

Montague felt silly. He still couldn't really believe that this was happening right now. That a complete stranger was speaking to him so candidly. But maybe that's precisely why he was opening up to this guy. There was no fear of judgment with a stranger. A stranger wasn't likely to call him "dumb" or a "halfwit."

Shit.

Montague *was* angry. He was really damn angry. Angry at all the years of abuse he'd had to put up with from his father.

And he was sad, too. Sad that he'd wasted all that time feeling like *he* was the one at fault.

He felt the strangest sensation—his eyes welled up with tears and he quickly blinked them away.

"It's all right," the man told him soothingly. "Go with it, son."

So that is what Montague did. He felt angry. He felt sad. He felt like totally fucking shit. And he didn't try to push the emotions away. His shoulders shook as he cried for the first time since he was a little boy.

"We're all little inside," the man whispered across to him.

Montague wiped his eyes, amazed by how much better he felt.

"And what about what makes you happiest?" the man asked, smiling. The man who–now he thought about it–looked more and more like his father. But like, the good version. The Guardian Angel version. The Fairy Godfather version.

"Oh, that's easy," said Montague. "That's Daisy." Then, another first: he smiled wide from ear-to-ear.

"Very good," said the man. "So...focus on Daisy. Everything else can eff off, pardon my *français*."

Montague nodded. "You're right, old man," he told the guy. "You know, you should do this for a living."

"Careful," he replied. "Grumps like you aren't meant to joke."

For the rest of the plane ride, Montague composed Daisy an email. It was a long message, explaining everything. He spoke about his father and his wife and all the things he hadn't yet managed to tell his babygirl in person. He apologized for leaving her last night and told her how much he regretted it. He promised her that he'd make amends. That this was just the start of something much bigger and much more wonderful. That, above all else, she could completely trust him not to be an asshole anymore.

By the time the plane landed, the email was finished. But just as he hit send something flew into his inbox.

It was an email from Daisy.

I should never have left my ex. We're getting back together.

What the...?

Shit.

Daisy must have been so miserable to send an email as abrupt as that. No emoticons. Not even her usual sign-off about glitter and sparkles. He'd fucked up by abandoning her like this. He'd really fucking fucked up.

Practically running off the plane, he called Daisy the second he reached the terminal building. But there was no answer.

CHAPTER 15 - DAISY

The words to "It's a Small World" had never sounded so creepy.

Daisy had run away from Raymond, and in an attempt to seek safety, she'd stepped into a line for a ride that she'd normally have loved. Three hundred cute little dolls singing about universal harmony against a glittery *papier-mâché* backdrop. Perfection.

But no.

Raymond had pushed past several families to get into the line beside her, and as they sailed in the boat together, she stole a look down at the ominous black water beneath them. Would he try to push her into the water? Surely there were safety protocols in place for something like that. They'd stop the ride and come to her rescue. People didn't *die* at Disneyland.

"I'm not marrying you, Raymond," she said for the zillionth time as the dolls sung about the tiny world they lived in. "I've moved on. You need to do the same."

"Moved on?" asked Raymond. "You found someone else?"

Daisy shook her head. It was a good thing the ride was dark so he wouldn't be able to see her cheeks burning. In the time since she'd run away from the altar, she *had* found someone else. She'd been spanked by him, bared her pussy for him, sucked his big, thick dick, and then been dumped by him, all in the space of a week.

Raymond didn't say anything else, but when Daisy turned around at the end of the ride, she saw that Raymond was secretly scrolling through her phone.

"Hey," she said crossly. "How'd you get into that?"

"I know your passcode, dufus," he told her. "It's the year President Truman ordered the development of the hydrogen bomb: 1950."

Daisy normally liked random facts, but she hated every single random fact that came out of Raymond's mouth. Besides, that wasn't the reason for her passcode. 1950 was the year that Disney's *Cinderella* first came out.

"Give me back my phone right now," Daisy hissed as they left the ride.

Ignoring her and still scrolling, Raymond asked: "What's a 'hand chair'?"

Oh no. That was a work email from Montague, alluding—albeit subtly—to what had happened between them in his office.

"It's nothing," Daisy said. "Just a work email from my boss. Give it back to me."

Raymond held the phone high in the air so Daisy couldn't reach. "How come you replied to his email with a winky face? You didn't write anything except a winky face."

Daisy looked around. There *had* to be a security guard around here somewhere. She swore she'd seen tons of them since she got here.

When she turned back to Raymond, she saw that he was writing something on her phone.

"What are you doing now?" she asked.

"Nothing you need to worry about, little lady," he told her. *Little lady.* Ugh. She should have liked being called "little", but not when it was Raymond. And not in that tone of voice.

"That's weird," said Raymond. "Your boss just sent you an email. Does he always use the words 'lick' and 'pussy' in his work emails?"

"Let me see!" Daisy cried, reaching out. "That's private."

"Daisy-doo, there are to be no secrets from us if this is going to work," Raymond told her, grabbing her wrist so hard that she cried out, tugging her in the direction of Davy Crockett's ranch.

"It will never, ever work between us," Daisy said, sighing with frustration. She just wanted this to be over now. She didn't want to have to make a fuss or make this any harder than it already was. Raymond was clearly in pain. She just wanted it to be over. For good. "Give me back my phone," she pleaded, "and we'll meet for coffee when we're back in Connecticut. We'll talk over all my reasons for leaving you." She really didn't want to meet for coffee. She really didn't want to see Raymond ever again. But if that's what it took...

"You know, we could sue your boss for sexual harassment," said Raymond, ignoring her. "We'd never have to worry about money again." He dragged her even harder now.

Daisy stopped, twisting Raymond's wrist into what her peers at school used to call a *snake bite*.

"Quit it," Raymond snarled, dragging her farther forward again. "We can't miss our second wedding. That'd be bad luck." He was still looking at her phone—looked like he was Googling something now.

"I don't know how many ways to tell you this, Raymond," said Daisy. "I'm. Not. Marrying. You."

Raymond stopped, still holding onto her wrist. "If you don't marry me," he said darkly, "something terrible will happen."

Daisy narrowed her eyes. "What do you mean? Are you threatening me?"

Raymond sighed, a pathetic expression appearing on his face. "I can't write a word without you, Daisy-doo," he whined. "I can't exist without you. You're my muse. My assistant. My everything. But the moment we get married, life will be good again. I'll publish my books. You'll have everything you ever wanted."

Daisy felt a pang of sadness for this poor, desperate man in front of her. Not because she liked him, but because of how deluded he was. Did he honestly believe that a wedding was going to fix all of his problems? His problems ran deep. Like, *super* deep. He needed years of therapy. And *she* needed a restraining order.

Raymond's expression changed all of a sudden. He looked up from Daisy's phone, a look of vindication in his eyes.

"This boss of yours..." he began. "You know he's a married man, right?"

What?

CHAPTER 16 - MONTAGUE

———————

Montague's lawyer, Owain, beckoned him into the board room. He was a miserable-looking man at the best of times, but right now he looked even more unhappy than usual. Sort of like a depressed ferret.

"Montague," he said. His beady black eyes flitted around, never quite resting on Montague's. The man was afraid of eye contact, but then he seemed to be afraid of everything. Montague hoped that wasn't going to be *him* in another ten years. "Thank god you're here…It's worse than we thought."

"What is?" asked Montague moodily, slumping into a chair at the head of the table.

"Your…situation, sir."

Montague could hardly be bothered to engage. He'd rushed straight here from the airport, he was severely jet-lagged, he hadn't slept in two days, and Daisy had just ended things before they even began. What was the point anymore? He was tempted to just give the whole damn lot to his ex-wife and sail away on his houseboat forever after. Start a new life as a fisherman or a… scarf knitter. Hell, he didn't know what kinds of jobs people on houseboats had. But he'd find out soon enough.

"I don't see how my situation could get any worse," Montague told Owain.

Owain selected a piece of paper from a massive pile on the table in front of him and slid it over to Montague. "It's rather delicate, sir," he warned. "The copywriter who quit a couple weeks ago? She's accusing you of sexual harassment. This could spell trouble for your divorce settlement too, I'm afraid, since the courts will see you as a womaniz—"

"She *what*?"

"It's all on the paper there, sir. Might be best for you to read it. I'm not sure I'm entirely comfortable reading some of those sentences aloud."

Montague looked at the paper in front of him, revolted by the things he was being accused of. There was no way that he'd done any of these things. He was all for the Me Too movement, and for women speaking up about discrimination in all kinds of areas including the workplace. And he was *entirely* up for looking at his own behaviors and reflecting on areas where he could improve. But this...it was just lies.

"You look incredulous, sir," said Owain.

"None of it's true."

"So you never had a relationship with this woman?"

Montague shifted uncomfortably. "I slept with her once. But it was about ten years ago. Long before either of us worked for this company—before this company existed. It was a one-off thing and neither of us was interested in it going further. A drunken one-night stand. She made the move on me, if I recall. It was well before I got married."

"It does make things a little messy, though," said Owain, looking more ferret-like than ever. "Trying to prove that it only happened that one time. It would have been easier if it had never happened at all."

Montague sighed. He was fed up of his past relationships coming back to haunt him. He just wanted a clean break with someone he cared about. And someone who cared about him, if such a thing was possible.

Obviously, it wasn't possible with Daisy.

But maybe one day he'd manage to forget about her, and he'd meet someone else he actually gave a damn about.

Yeah, right.

"You're sure that everything else she's saying is a lie?" Owain asked.

"Of course it is," Montague said. "I'd never do *that* with a safety pin." He looked at what was written on the paper and shuddered. "Look. I guess I wasn't too nice to Penny in the last couple months."

"She only worked at the company a couple months."

"Thing is, I haven't been too nice to *anyone* lately. I guess I created something of a toxic workplace. Maybe this is her revenge."

CHAPTER 16 - MONTAGUE

As he read, he saw that Penny was alleging that he had only agreed to hire her because they'd slept together. Which wasn't true in the least. Sam from HR had hired her because she was a good copywriter. Montague had disclosed the past encounter on the HR form, as was office policy. *She* hadn't disclosed it, but agreed that it had happened when Sam pressed her.

"And what about the matter with your wife, sir?" asked Owain. "This really is a lot, you know. Trouble with your wife and an employee. It's not going to go down well with the courts *or* the public. Especially in...your line of work. How are you going to deal with it all?"

Montague growled. "You're my lawyer. Why are you asking me? Isn't it *your* job to sort this out?"

Owain made a small, ferrety noise. "Is there anything else I should know about? Any other secret that might come out of the closet at an inopportune moment? I have my work cut out for me here."

Montague put his head in his hands. "I'm screwed. Maybe I *am* a terrible person. I obviously really upset this woman. I upset all my staff here by being a grump. I've been trying to remedy it, but...maybe it's all just too fucking late."

Owain looked over Montague's shoulder, presumably taking in the snack wagon, the nap corner, the juice station, the trampoline, the laughing staff members, and the general feeling of frivolity in the office.

"If you're a grump," said Owain, "then I wish I worked for someone way, way grumpier."

Montague sighed. "What's the point of trying to change if the whole world's against me?"

"If you search within your heart and really don't think you did this, sir," said Owain, "then you need to fight it. Just like you need to fight your wife. It's not normal in a divorce case for the wife to get ninety-nine percent of everything. There's no way she'll get it. But if you're saying that she coerced you into the marriage under false pretenses, then we can't let her have a dime."

"Nobody will believe me she lied about the pregnancy, though," said Montague. "It's her word against mine." He sighed yet again. "And now that the copywriter's saying shit about me, I haven't got a hope in hell of being believed."

Owain handed over two full files of paper. "Read over what they're both saying. Go over every word with a fine-tooth comb. Then we'll talk."

"Right," said Montague, shaking his head. He should have been in Disneyland with Daisy right now. He should have been signing the contract and making his vows. Real, meaningful vows like: *I promise to never lie. I promise to listen. I promise to give you my full heart.*

"I'll call you tonight," said Owain. "Happy reading, sir."

Owain left and Montague did what the man on the plane had told him. He let himself feel angry, sad, the whole shebang.

Montague's house felt so big and empty.

For a man who'd felt like he never had any time, it suddenly felt like he had all the time in the world. But what use was time if you had nobody to share it with?

He looked at the piles of documents in front of him. Accusations. Lies. Hatred. Pure misery.

For that brief period he'd been with Daisy, the storm cloud over his head had started to dissipate. He'd noticed colors shine brighter, food taste better, his heart begin to thaw. Now, all that goodness had been washed down the drain. The storm cloud was back, and it was bigger than ever.

As he read sentence after sentence describing what a bad man he was, the words began flying around the page. He yawned, rubbing his eyes. It was only lunchtime, but he needed sleep. He couldn't let himself, though. Not when he had a mess as big as this to sort out.

He was even starting to see things. The two women's reports were starting to merge together into one. It looked as though they both had the same address.

Wait.

Both women *did* have the same address.

What the hell?

CHAPTER 16 - MONTAGUE

Montague felt a glimmer of hope inside of him, like a tiny ember was being fanned deep in his ribcage, and slowly turning into a flame.

Just then, his phone rang. It was Sam, his HR guy.

"Boss," he said. "We need to talk." His voice sounded strange. Shaky. As if there was some sort of emotion bubbling beneath the surface.

"Make it quick," Montague said.

So Sam *did*. Angrily, he asked: "What's all this stuff about Daisy?"

He froze. "What are you talking about?"

"Sir," said Sam, no longer bothering to hide his anger. "Did something inappropriate happen between you in Paris?"

Montague swallowed.

The ember in his heart was extinguished.

CHAPTER 17 - DAISY

Raymond had messed up throughout their entire relationship. Thankfully, he'd messed up again. Turned out he hadn't booked a wedding at the Davy Crockett Ranch. He'd booked a table for two at Crockett's Tavern. Daisy had no idea how he'd done that, but she didn't care. All that mattered was that she hadn't had to marry him today, and she considered that a win.

Daisy had gotten good at looking on the bright side over the last few years. Unfortunately, in this instance, the bright side wasn't *that* bright.

Raymond now had more than just her phone. He also had her passport and the company credit card. The way he'd gotten them? Blackmail. And now, it was blackmail that he was using to make things even worse.

"You won't regret this, little lady," he said, slurping his Frappuccino. "I'll make things right this time. We'll marry, we'll have ten kids, and I'm seriously so close to finishing this novel. This is the one, Daisy-doo. We'll be on easy street once this gets picked up." He paused. "Thank god we're back together, my love. I'd be nothing without you. I'd kill myself the second you walked away."

Daisy sat glumly looking at her coffee. Raymond had ordered her a decaf. Told her it was time she kicked her flighty habit. Said that maybe caffeine was the reason she'd left him in the first place. She was too restless—always had been.

Right now, they were sitting outside the world's most beloved bookstore, Shakespeare and Co. Daisy wasn't a massive literature buff or anything, but she enjoyed a good novel from time to time, and seeing all those books in the window of the store should have been exciting. It should have been romantic. Instead, it was yet more sadness in a life that had already caused her to suffer so much.

Since leaving Disneyland this morning, Raymond had given Daisy more information about Montague. He was married to a performance artist named Olga Kozlov. Five months ago, she'd filed a harassment case against him. Apparently, he'd gotten her pregnant then left her when she miscarried, and now he won't give her any money.

There was another case against him too. Penny Freeman, his old copywriter, claimed that Montague had only hired her because they slept together, and once she started working at the company, he pressured her to have sex. When she told him she wasn't interested, he embarked on a series of abusive acts, including sticking a safety pin into her crotch as punishment. She quit out of fear for her life.

Daisy couldn't believe how wrong she'd been about Montague. She'd known that he had his bad points, obviously, but she had also felt that, deep down, he was a good man. It all made sense now, though. The way he'd invited her over to his house so late at night. She'd fallen asleep on the couch, then woken up in one of his bedrooms—had he drugged her and done something to her while she slept? Is that why he'd taken her shopping the following morning? A way of making amends for his sins?

Then there was the spanking at work. Not exactly legit.

Tying her to his bed in Paris and sticking his cock down her throat. Which, now she thought about it, was pretty selfish of him. If anyone had deserved to get off that night, it had been *her*.

Oh, man. She'd made the same mistake again. Trying to see the best in someone. Convincing herself that someone was a good person when they were actually a giant a-hole.

And yet...it hadn't felt bad at the time. It felt good. *So* good.

Dang it. None of that mattered now.

Raymond had told Daisy that she had to marry him or he'd throw himself in the Seine, and it'd be all her fault.

Obviously, Daisy was still hoping for an escape plan. Apparently, they couldn't legally marry in France without giving ten days' notice. Ten days was a long time. Daisy was bound to think of a way out of all this before time was up. Plus, she had ten days to try to bring Raymond to his senses. To make him see that she didn't want to marry him, but that he definitely shouldn't kill himself.

"Man, it's gonna be so good living here," said Raymond, smoking a disgusting menthol cigarette. "Cheap red wine, cigarettes, and coffee. Just like the old writers from the 1920s."

"I don't think they drank Frappuccinos in the 1920s," snapped Daisy. She was so sticky and hot in this humid weather. All she wanted to do was flop down on her hotel bed and put on some Disney movies and try to get her sunshine back.

Raymond chose to ignore her remark. "I'll get a beat-up old typewriter and finish my novel on it. You can support us by waiting tables again." He grinned. "I've heard the saucy bars pay well if you take off your clothes."

Daisy swallowed. "I'm not going to do that."

"I guess you don't need to find a job immediately," said Raymond. "We have your company credit card for now. I'm sure your boss won't mind us having a little fun." He blew a smoke ring, then punctured it with his forefinger. "After all, he hasn't got much choice with the threat of even more court action hanging over him."

Daisy felt her blood run cold. "You threatened him?"

Raymond smiled. "Let's just say I planted a seed."

"What does that mean?"

"What's going on between you two is hardly appropriate, is it?" Raymond said. "Babe, you got Harvey Weinsteined. That fuckwit deserves everything that's coming to him."

"So wait," Daisy said. "I'm confused. Have you already threatened him? Or are you spending the company money for ten days, *then* threatening him? Because I'm pretty sure we'd get in trouble with the police if we—"

"Chill out, little lady," said Raymond. "Let Daddy take care of it. That's what you like, right? Daddy stuff? Always thought you were childish and a bit perverted. But you know what, fuck it. Whatever floats your boat. If it means I get to keep you, then I'll be your Daddy. And you can be my tiny little lady, sucking Daddy's cock all day long."

"You've got it all wrong. It's not like that. And I *definitely* don't want you to be my Daddy."

Raymond's icy expression melted slightly. "Daisy-doo, I know you don't trust me yet. But I'm doing all of this in your best interest. You need me, just like I need you. Someone as sweet and innocent as you...It would be all too easy for you to... go down the wrong path. I don't want that for you. I want you to be safe."

Daisy's head reeled. She felt like she was back in Connecticut, trapped in the old patterns. Raymond's constant cycle of threats, affection, promises, more threats, more promises. It was enough to drive anyone out of their minds. It made her question herself, and her own reality. It was gaslighting, pure and simple. She knew that. Over the years, she'd gotten good at recognizing it.

But unfortunately, that didn't really help her situation. In fact, it just made everything feel even more hopeless.

"You look a little down, babe," Raymond observed. "Let's go indulge in some retail therapy. Typewriter for me, Little French maid outfit for you—"

"No," Daisy snapped. "No to all of it."

But even as she said those words, she found herself standing up and following Raymond. Because what else could she do? She was trapped in a foreign country with a mentally unstable man. And, unlike Cinderella, she had no Prince Charming to save her.

CHAPTER 18 – MONTAGUE

It had been a long time since he'd stood outside this address—Olga's place.

She lived in the Miami Design district, a bustling area full of hipster art galleries and trendy restaurants. She had a loft apartment in a building that looked like it was covered in bullet holes. Of course, that was just a design feature.

Montague remembered the first time he'd visited this place. How cool he thought it was. Now, he just found it pretentious. There was nothing edgy about bullet holes and blood and gore. It was just a bunch of artists preying on people's fears for money.

He pushed the buzzer for Olga's place, but there was no answer. Damn. It was hot out here today, and muggy as hell. According to weather reports, a storm was due. Storm Tremaine–likely to affect the entire northern hemisphere. Probably a good thing, to take the edge off this humidity. Montague already had huge sweat patches on his t-shirt. He should have brought some water with him.

He sat on a bench under a covered area on the sidewalk, wondering how long he should wait before giving up. If it wasn't so damn uncomfortable out here, he'd be tempted to wait as long as it took. He needed to get to the bottom of all this, and if Olga wasn't answering his calls, then this was the only way. His lawyer wouldn't be happy, but screw it. He wasn't going to sit by and let his life be dismantled like this.

Sam's call had rattled him. Apparently, Daisy hadn't given any details, but she'd emailed Sam to tell him that there had been an "inappropriate event" at the hotel last night. When she felt ready, she said, she'd reveal everything.

Obviously, Montague had replayed the "inappropriate event" she was referring to a thousand times in his head since then, trying to figure out how he could have upset her so badly. They had a safeword. She'd been wet as hell,

145

practically begging him to fuck her.

Had it all been an act?

The more he thought about it, the more sure he was that Daisy was a fake.

No woman *that* perfect would really be into him. She was beautiful. Sweet. Funny. It was like she'd been designed to please him. An artist's rendition of a perfect partner.

Daisy, he decided, was Olga's creation.

After all, she had come into his life at *exactly* the time that Olga was trying to steal everything he owned. And now that he knew that Penny and Olga lived at the same address, everything had crystallized for him. Penny and Olga were in on this together–lying about him in order to squeeze every last cent from his pockets. And they'd employed Daisy, too. Probably paying her off with something of his–the cabin at Lake Tahoe, maybe–when this was all done. Three women against one man. They'd destroy him.

Unless he took affirmative action.

He sweated and waited, growing thirstier and hungrier by the minute. When did he last eat? Maybe not since Paris. Fuck. He needed to put an end to all this crap. He just wanted to get on with his life. Run his business in peace. If he couldn't make himself happy, then at least he could try and keep his staff happy. That was an okay life, right?

Time dragged on. Time, time, time.

What use was time to him when he had nobody to spend it with?

As he watched endless streams of hipsters walking past him, a familiar face appeared in the crowd. It wasn't Olga, though. It was Penny.

Never mind. Penny would do. In fact, she might even be better.

He jumped up, immediately becoming a little light-headed in the heat. Damn. He needed to hydrate.

"Penny!" he called out.

Immediately, her expression changed. Her eyes widened, and she froze on the spot.

"I-I, er," she stammered. "I'm not supposed to talk to you."

He held up his hands. "I just want to talk, Penny," he said. "I was here looking for Olga. But I'd like to talk to you too. Is that okay? We could go to someplace public. There's a coffee shop farther up the street?"

Penny hesitated but then nodded. "O-okay."

"Great." He was relieved. He could chat to Penny *and* get something to drink. You had to celebrate the little victories.

Penny was reluctant to chat on the way to the coffee shop, but she seemed to relax a little when he bought her a latte and a slice of carrot cake. He felt better, too, for ordering a glass of orange juice and a brownie.

As they took a booth sitting opposite one another, he couldn't help feeling bad for Penny. Even though she'd lied about him, she seemed so small, so scared. It was hard to believe, honestly, that the two of them had ever slept together. Penny hadn't aged well. She looked thin and twitchy, with bad teeth.

He hadn't noticed while she'd worked for him—he'd always been too wrapped up in his own affairs to pay much attention to his employees. But now that he thought about it, she looked a bit like...a junkie?

"So," Montague began. "How long have you known Olga?"

Penny shifted awkwardly in her seat, not seeming to like his question. She kept slipping her phone out her pocket and checking it, and looking around the room as though waiting for someone.

"I don't really know her too well..." Penny replied cagily. "I guess I just got to know her because we have some stuff in common."

Like you're both lying to screw me over.

Montague felt his smartwatch buzz, telling him he was stressed. But it had been doing that for days now. This was an attempt to bring the stress levels back down. He wasn't going to let Olga give him a heart attack. He couldn't let that happen.

"What the hell are you doing, Monty?" asked an angry and all-too-familiar Russian voice behind him. "And you, Penny. You shouldn't be talking to him. You'll jeopardize the case!"

Penny flinched. "S-sorry."

"Time to leave," Olga said to Penny.

"I haven't finished my carrot cake," Penny said tremulously. "Can I at least get it boxed up?"

"No."

Penny scooted out of her seat and ran out the coffee shop, past all the trendy pot plants and mustachioed hipsters, and out into the street.

Olga sat in the booth in Penny's place. She took a bite of Penny's carrot cake, frosting and walnut crumbs briefly coating her lips. She grimaced and pushed the plate away.

She looked terrible. Normally, she had a severe red bob with razor-sharp bangs. Today, her hair was scraped back in a short ponytail and frizzy from the humidity. Everything about her screamed: frazzled.

"What's going on here, Olga?" Montague asked. "This attempt to ruin me. Are you in trouble, or something?"

Olga laughed. "You're the one in trouble, Monty. Looks like I got you right where I want you."

"And where's that?"

"You have a sexual harassment lawsuit to deal with now," she replied coldly. "After the trial, you'll never work again."

Montague spoke through clenched teeth. "Why are you doing this to me?"

Olga sighed. "Because you left me when I was miscarrying."

"No, I didn't!" Montague cried, exasperated. A few people in the coffee shop looked around, so he lowered his voice. "You were never pregnant."

Olga shrugged. 'Potato, *potah-to*. You married me when I told you I was pregnant. Then you left me after you found out I wasn't pregnant anymore. It's the same difference."

"No it isn't," Montague replied. "You lied to me."

Olga smiled. "You don't get it, do you? There's someone else in the mix now. The copywriter. You—"

"I did nothing to her. Except acted a bit moody a couple times."

Olga tutted. "Oh, dear. In denial, are you?"

Montague narrowed his eyes. "You're lying again. You manipulated her into this. I don't know how you found her, or how you convinced her to join in with this charade—"

Olga grinned, then sniffed and rubbed her nose. "Let's just say we have things in common."

"What's that meant to—"

He was interrupted by the beep of his phone. He grabbed it out his pocket in a flash, hoping to see Daisy's name on his screen. Instead, it was a text from a number he didn't recognize. *What have you done to Daisy? She's in Paris and she's not answering our messages. If you've hurt her, I'll hurt you!*

What? If Daisy was in on this charade with Olga, then why was she still in Paris? And why wasn't she replying to her messages? A terrible thought hit him.

"What have you done with Daisy? You'd better not hurt her."

Olga frowned. "Daisy? Who's Daisy?"

"Don't lie to me," he said through gritted teeth. "You paid her to take part in your stupid revenge scheme, just like you paid Penny. And now you've done something to her, haven't you?" His face turned pale. "You promised her money, and now you don't want to pay her. You're evil, Olga. Pure evil."

Ignoring Olga's attempts at insulting him, he typed a message back. *Who is this?*

A reply came instantly: *It's Kiera. Daisy's friend. And there's something you should know. Her ex, Raymond, is out there too.*

Montague shot his response back: *It's okay. I think she wants to be with him now.*

Be with him? Kiera wrote. *The man's a lunatic. He'll kill her.*

Montague felt a stabbing sensation in his stomach. Suddenly, he thought about those messages he's received from Daisy. There had been no sunshine or rainbow emoticons, no smiley or winky faces. They hadn't seemed like Daisy at all. What if they...weren't?

"I'm outta here," he said, downing his juice and taking a huge bite out of his brownie.

"Leaving so soon?" said Olga with a smile. "I was starting to enjoy myself."

Montague looked at her pityingly. "People I care about need me. From now on, I'm going to use my time wisely."

He tried to stand up, but his blood was whooshing in his ears. Then, his heart started to race. It became difficult to swallow. His abdomen began cramping.

It was Olga's turn to look pitying now. "Oh, dear," she said. "Looks like you need to watch what you put in that dirty mouth of yours."

As he gasped for air, he gripped the edge of the table. And that's when he saw his plate. He hadn't just taken a bite of his brownie at all. Olga had swapped the plates around. He'd taken a huge bite of Penny's carrot cake, walnuts and all.

"Oops," said Olga, sniffing and twitching again.

Montague's legs buckled and he hit the floor. He looked up at Olga, desperate for help, but knowing that she wouldn't give it to him. From his position on the floor, he noticed something. Her red nostrils, crusted with white powder.

Of course.

Olga and Penny were both addicts.

They wanted everything he had to fuel their addiction.

He gasped again, and his smartwatch buzzed to tell him he was in danger. All kinds of images began flashing in front of him.

His bullying father, telling him he'd never amount to anything.

His miserable mother, sobbing and broken.

Daisy, in trouble and in need of him.

Olga looked down at him. "I'll save you if you promise me I win." She sneered. Olga the addict. What was her poison? Coke? Crack? Heroin? He hoped it was fucking worth it.

Thinking about drugs reminded him of something. His EpiPen. He'd never had to use it before, but of course he always carried it. He reached into his pocket, grabbed the syringe, and then thrust it deep into his thigh.

The next breath he took was the first breath of a new life. The old Montague was gone now. The new Montague had been born. And he meant fucking business.

CHAPTER 19 - DAISY

Finally, Raymond was snoring. He always started snoring the moment he hit deep sleep. Daisy knew that because whenever Raymond was snoring, it was almost impossible to wake him. Over the years, she'd prodded him, pushed him, and even yelled at him, but there was never any way to make the snoring stop.

The rest of the time, Raymond was a light sleeper. Like, super light. He'd blame Daisy for giving him a bad night's sleep if she tossed and turned too much, got up to pee, opened a door too loud, or even smacked her lips together.

Thankfully, though, he was sleeping like a baby right now. He'd insisted that they sleep in the Presidential Suite that Montague had slept in last night. It had felt really weird and wrong lying on the mattress with Raymond in the very spot that she'd sucked Montague's cock just twenty-four hours earlier.

Of course, she hadn't touched him. She had slept with all her clothes on, curled up in a ball.

Raymond was a lot of bad things, but he wasn't the kind of guy who'd force himself on someone sexually. He'd respected Daisy's wishes when she told him that she didn't want to have sex. Well, maybe "respected" wasn't the right word. He'd tolerated her wishes, but told her that he was confident that she'd be sleeping with him by the end of the week.

Yeah, right.

Daisy had finally come up with an escape plan. And now that Raymond was snoring, it was time to put it into action.

She slipped out from under the blankets, wishing that she had her Fairy Godmother pillowcase. It was still on the pillow in her adjoining room. That thing always gave her luck. Or, at least, it felt good to hold it like a comforter when she felt afraid. She didn't have time to get it now, though. She couldn't risk waking Raymond.

She grabbed her glasses from the bedside table then tiptoed across the luxuriously carpeted floor. She loved this carpet–right now it was a blessing as it helped muffle the sound of her footsteps.

Next, she needed to get the hotel key out of Raymond's jeans. They were slung over the back of the chair, and the big brass buckle of his belt clanged a little as she rifled through the pockets. Luckily, she found the key card without too much hassle. Then, she crept into the living room and all the way to the front door, where she'd lined up her sneakers in anticipation of this moment.

Shoes on. She opened and shut the door excruciatingly slowly, to make the process as close to silent as possible. Then...

Release.

She was out in the corridor, heading down to the hotel foyer.

Unfortunately, this wasn't the kind of hotel that had a computer in the reception area for public use. People here used their extremely expensive laptops or smartphones or instructed staff members to send messages for them. But hers wasn't the kind of message she wanted just anyone to hear.

So, she left the hotel in search of an internet café. The moment she stepped outside, she was surprised by the weather. It wasn't just raining—it was *pouring*. Felt like an all-out storm.

"Dang it," she muttered under her breath. She hadn't thought to bring her coat out with her, and getting wet like this threatened to completely ruin her plan.

Daisy's escape plan was not a straightforward one. Raymond had stowed away her passport and phone in a locker at the train station and he was keeping the key in a little pouch in his underpants. Fishing around in his jeans pocket while he was asleep was one thing. There was *no way* she was fishing about in his underpants pouch. Just. No. Way.

Her plan, then, was to fire off an email to Kiera and Peach, to tell them of her whereabouts. Then, she would head back to the hotel and get back into bed as though nothing was amiss. Connecticut was six hours behind Paris, so hopefully, they'd still be up, and they could start working out a way to come rescue her.

Obviously getting back into bed dripping wet from the rain wasn't ideal. She'd have to pretend she'd taken a midnight shower...fully clothed.

As she hurried past all the luxury boutiques on Avenue Montaigne, she was on the lookout for someplace to go. She had two euros in her pocket which she'd been lucky enough to find on the sidewalk at Disney World this morning. She'd always known it was a magical place. She just hoped two euros would be enough.

Three blocks from the hotel, she spotted a yellow sign down an alley. "Le CyberCafé." Underneath: "*24 heures sur 24.*" She was no expert in French, but she was pretty sure that this was exactly what she needed. Keeping her head ducked down as she rushed through the rain, she raced for it.

Inside the internet café, she stole a look behind her as she entered and was relieved that there was nobody following her.

There was a large man reading a comic at a desk near the door, and he grunted at her when she entered. Behind him, there were two rows of old-looking monitors and a couple of people sat clicking away at computer games with what looked like cold cups of coffee beside them. She wished she could afford a coffee. Her head was throbbing from the lack of caffeine today.

She was about to ask the comic guy the cost of using the internet, but without looking up, he pointed to a sign on his desk. "1 euro a minute." Okay. She could definitely understand that. She had precisely two minutes to save her skin.

She sat at the nearest computer, wiping the lenses of her rain-spattered glasses on her pajama pants. She was wearing Disney pajamas but hey, this was Paris. She felt certain that you could get away with wearing Disney pajamas in a city as forward-thinking as this. And anyway, what choice did she have?

She put her two euros in the coin slot.

Right. Here goes.

One of the coins tumbled out of the slot so she tried posting it in again.

It tumbled out again.

Shoot.

"Excuse me?" she called.

The guy reading the comic book didn't react.

There was already a timer on the screen counting down from a minute. She had fifty-two seconds left. She could spend those fifty-two seconds trying to resolve the issue with her second euro, or she could use the time she had and hope for the best. No time to decide. She had to just try and make this work.

She opened up her email, typing her address and password as quickly as she could possibly manage, hoping she didn't make any typos. Thankfully, she didn't. Her email opened up and she was overjoyed to see Peach and Kiera were on the group chat.

Guys! she typed. *Ray took my passport. I'm trapped in Paris! Can't get home. Need rescue!*

No job's too big, no pup's too small! replied Peach.

Cute, but Daisy didn't have time for PAW-Patrol-related cuteness right now.

Where exactly R U? replied Kiera. *Your phone says you've been at the train station for hours.*

Daisy replied with the name of the hotel.

She could see the three dots that meant that Kiera was typing something.

Then the dots disappeared.

They appeared again.

"Come on, Kiera!" she whispered. "Hurry up!"

Red digits began flashing on the screen. *5...4...3...2...*

Dude! Go straight to the—

The screen went black.

Daisy put her second euro in the slot another time, and it fell out again. She ran over to the comic book guy.

"I need another minute! My euro's not working!"

The guy looked at her as though waking from a dream, confused and still half asleep. He took the euro out of her hand and frowned at it. "*Ce n'est pas bien,*" he said, then grumpily added: "No good."

154

CHAPTER 19 - DAISY

"Why not?" she asked.

"Souvenir," he replied.

She looked at the coin more closely now and realized what it was. It was a Disneyland Paris souvenir coin. There was a picture of Mickey on one side, and Cinderella's castle on the other. All right, so technically it was a Sleeping Beauty castle at Disneyland, but that didn't matter to Daisy. This coin was clearly a sign from the universe.

Everything was going to be okay!

Slipping the coin safely into her pajama pocket, she ran out into the rain. She felt a little vulnerable in her pajamas, just as she had before, but she kept to the well-lit streets as much as possible. As she ran, she suddenly knew exactly where she was headed. Peach was the one who had inspired her. There was no PAW Patrol in Paris. Well, not the *real* PAW Patrol. But there *were* police.

Of course. She should have thought about this before. She'd been so caught up in trying to be rescued that she hadn't thought about saving herself. She didn't have to wait for a security guard at Disneyland, or her friends, or even her Fairy Godmother. She had everything she needed right here. She had *herself*. And she was perfectly capable of effecting her own rescue, thank you very much!

A sudden clap of thunder nearly made her jump out of her skin, and she started running faster.

But finding a police station wasn't as easy as she'd hoped it would be. She tried to think back to her French lessons at school. What was the French word for police? She'd need to stop and ask for directions in a hotel, or a bodega, or —

"I was worried," said a familiar voice as bony fingers encircled her wrist like handcuffs. "You started sleepwalking, toots?"

Toots?

She turned at the same moment as a crack of lightning lit up the whole sky, lighting up Raymond's ghostly face with it.

"I, er..." she mumbled. "No. I..." She sighed. "Yes."

Raymond looked down at her shoes doubtfully. He yanked her along the sidewalk back toward the hotel. "I rolled over in my sleep and found you gone. I was so scared, honey."

Honey, now? What's with all these never-used-before nicknames?

"Almost threw myself off the balcony when I saw you'd gone," Raymond told her. "Thought life wasn't worth living." He pulled her inside the hotel lobby, wrapping her in his coat. "Glad I got you back." He paused. "We can keep each other safe, huh?"

Daisy had always been superstitious about using elevators during lightning storms and Raymond knew that, but he pulled her inside of it before she had a chance to protest. She should have shouted out for help in the lobby, but for some reason, she felt so shocked to be back in Raymond's clutches that she couldn't get the words out.

Back in the room, Raymond pushed Daisy onto the bed, wet pajamas and all, then he took his belt and tied her wrists to the bedposts, just as Montague had done.

Just as Montague had, except for a few key differences.

Number one: no consent.

Number two: no safeword.

Number three: no fun. Only fear.

"I feel inspired," Raymond said, taking a seat at the desk and removing the lid from the top-of-the-range typewriter he'd bought earlier in the day. "Always did prefer writing late at night. And the thunderstorm makes everything so exciting, don't you think?" He began to hit at the keys.

Daisy thrashed and wriggled. "Let me go!"

Raymond turned to her with wide, innocent eyes. "But darling, I don't want you running off in your sleep again, do I? Anything could happen."

"At least let me change out of these wet clothes. And I want my pillow from the other room. I can't sleep well without it."

Of course, there was no way in hell she was about to sleep, but she did want her comforter all the same.

Raymond turned, screwed his nose up at her in disgust, then walked off into the adjoining room. He returned with the Fairy Godmother pillow and

156

threw it at her. It landed on her face, and she thrashed about to get free of it before it suffocated her.

"Let me go, Raymond," she said, louder now.

"Nuh-uh," said Raymond, sitting at his typewriter again. "You're my muse. I need my muse. When I finish this new novel, you'll be so proud of me. It'll be a huge success. We'll have everything we ever wanted and more."

He was raving like he'd completely lost it. Raymond had always been a bit...much, but this was something else.

"You know, it's a good thing you ran out on our last wedding," he said. "This is so much more romantic, don't you think?"

Daisy thrashed about some more, but it was no use. The belt was buckled so tightly around her wrists, she could already feel the dark bruises forming there.

Raymond turned back to the typewriter, hitting the keys with a manic energy. She hated to think what he was writing about. His novels were all kinda...horrible. About madmen whose lives spiraled out of control until they invariably went on killing sprees. He described them as literary thrillers, but Daisy had come to think of them more as fantasy. Not fantasy like dragons and unicorns. Fantasy like Raymond was writing out his darkest fantasies on the page, experimenting with all the things he was trying to hold himself back from doing in real life.

"How long are you planning on keeping me here?" Daisy asked. "I bet if I scream, I'll wake up the guests, and they'll send the staff running in immediately."

Raymond shook his head. "They insulate suites like this very well. Ain't nobody gonna hear me and you, babe, no matter *what* we get up to."
He looked over at her, a greedy glint in his eye.

"Don't do this, Raymond," she pleaded. "At least let me dry off. I'm soaking the mattress. And this belt is too tight. It's hurting my wrists."

Raymond laughed a hollow laugh. "But this is what you're into, buttercup. Punishments and domination, right? I'm keeping the relationship alive."

"You're getting it all wrong," Daisy said, tears rolling down her cheeks. "I don't like this at all, Raymond. I'm scared."

Raymond narrowed his eyes at her. "What is it you Little people like, then? You like getting smacked? Is that what I'm forgetting?"

"Raymond, I feel like you're punishing me for not marrying you. I don't like it. Please stop."

"Nuh-uh." Raymond waggled a finger at her. "Baby's gonna get a spanky-wanky for being naughty-waughty."

Daisy felt sick to the stomach. This was everything that Daddy Dom Little Girl stuff was *not*. This was just...abuse.

Raymond walked over to her, looking down at her. He took a cigarette out his pocket and lit it.

Daisy glanced over at the no-smoking symbol on the wall. Something told her it wouldn't help if she pointed it out to him.

"I finally get why things didn't work between us last time," Raymond said through clenched teeth. "It's because you're a pervert. I saw an email your disgusting boss wrote to you this morning. I saw the way he talked to you."

"Montague wrote to me?" she asked. "What did he say?"

Raymond shrugged. "That's ancient history now."

Daisy's heart raced. She'd been so sure that he'd abandoned her, but what if he'd written explaining everything to her? What if he had a good excuse for leaving her here? On the other hand, maybe it was a break-up email. Or...worse than that...a plain old *work* email.

"You want to pretend to be a child and pretend that I'm your father," Raymond mocked, taking a step closer, "and you want me to hit you so hard you scream." He pulled down her rain-soaked pajama pants, revealing her white panties.

She kicked at him, but he caught her foot mid-air and laughed.

"Now, where's the most painful place to get spanked?" he asked her. "The sole of your foot? Your pussy?"

"No, no, no!" Daisy screamed as loud as her lungs would let her. It was a scream of fear, a scream of pain, but most of all a scream that wanted to be set free.

"Shut up," Raymond snarled. "I know I said these rooms are soundproofed, but there's my eardrums to consider." He took a drag of his cigarette, then looked down at her. "I know," he said. "Here's a bit of *predicament play* for you. If you scream again, I'll burn you with my cigarette." He grabbed her thigh and held the red end of the cigarette just inches from her skin.

"No, Raymond. Don't do that. I won't scream again. Just get that thing away from me."

He smiled. "I know. Maybe I'll burn your favorite pillowcase instead." He moved the cigarette across to the Fairy Godmother's face.

"Raymond. Please. Leave that alone."

He laughed, then took a long drag of the cigarette, blowing the smoke into Daisy's face. At the very same moment, an alarm sounded above them, and Daisy was hit by a torrent of falling water. Her first thought was that the ceiling had caved in—that the rain from the storm was pouring all over her. Then, when her eyes were able to focus again, she saw that the sprinkler system had gone off, triggered by Raymond's cigarette.

"Shit," he said. "My manuscript."

He dropped his cigarette and ran back toward his typewriter. Daisy could smell the pillowcase burning beside her before she could see it.

Please be okay, Fairy Godmother!

"Fuck," Raymond said. "My words!"

He started collecting sheets of sopping wet paper, cursing and huffing. As he did so, the flames right by Daisy's head seemed to be having a fight with the sprinkler system and winning. There was a new smell now. Charred and chemical. Bleachy.

"Raymond!" she screamed. "My hair's on fire! Help me!"

Suddenly, she heard the front door barge open, followed by heavy footsteps.

And then she saw him in the doorway. He was back. And he had a policeman with him.

Instantly, Raymond lifted his typewriter and hurled it at the policeman, who fell to the ground.

"It's over," Montague said to Raymond, his voice deep and commanding. He looked over at Daisy, instantly aghast when he saw the flames so close to her face. He ran over to her and threw the blanket over the fire.

"Montague!" Daisy yelled, looking behind him. "He's going to hit you!"

Quick as a flash, Montague reached for something in his pocket and jabbed it behind him.

Raymond dropped to the floor with a shout of anguish.

Montague didn't even bother to look. "Well, how about that?" he said. "Haven't used a damn EpiPen for two decades, then all of a sudden I use it twice in two days." He continued to tend to Daisy, unbuckling her wrists and making sure there were no flames left.

"Will it kill him?" Daisy asked nervously.

"Nah," Montague said. "It's just a nice, big shot of adrenaline. He'll be fine."

Daisy nodded, her eyes flooding with fresh tears.

"Sweetheart," he said, holding her in his arms. "I'm so sorry I left you."

"It's okay, Daddy," she sobbed into his shoulder. "It must have been very important."

"Actually, no," he said, stroking her back, moving her out of the jet of the sprinkler. "Nothing in this world is important as you. I know that now."

Raymond, who had been moaning on the floor, was starting to get up again, but fortunately, so was the policeman. He clipped his wrists with handcuffs, and Raymond whined.

"You stole my wife, asshole!"

Montague raised an eyebrow at him. "Let's ask Daisy what she wants, shall we?" He turned to her. "Daisy, do you want this man?"

"No, I don't," Daisy sobbed. "I want *you*."

Montague nodded. "I want you too, babygirl." He looked deep into her eyes. "I love you."

Her heart did backflips. Backflips that could only mean one thing. It was the feeling she'd been waiting for her whole life long, but she'd never known that until right now. "I love you too, Daddy."

Raymond was about to say something, but the policeman led him away. They listened to him screaming about wanting his manuscript and his typewriter back, but the policeman didn't seem to care.

Just then, the sprinkler system shut off, and the room was quiet again. Montague brushed Daisy's hair behind her ears. "You can forget about him now, little mouse," he said softly. "He's committed several offenses in the last few days alone. Kidnap. Theft. Physical abuse. Credit card fraud."

Daisy pushed her face into Montague's chest, crying softly. "I'm sorry, Daddy."

"No," Montague told her. "I'm sorry. I never should have left you. I'd like to explain it to you, to make it up to you. But...whaddya say we get out of this room first? Too many memories, I think, don't you?"

Daisy nodded. "Yeah. Maybe. But...my Fairy Godmother." She looked over at her pillowcase, bracing herself for the worst. But...it was a miracle. Her pillowcase hadn't burned at all. Just the hotel blankets.

"It's magic," she whispered, running her hands over it.

Montague touched her shoulder. "You don't have to talk about any of this until you're ready, okay? For now, I just want to look after you. If you'll let me."

"I will," Daisy replied.

Montague did something Daisy had never seen him do before. He smiled. And then, right after the smile, he kissed her.

CHAPTER 20 - MONTAGUE

"What do you think of the view, little mouse?" Daisy asked her new stuffie.

They hadn't been able to sleep after everything that had happened, so after they'd given the police their statements, they'd walked the streets of Paris until sunrise. Daisy hadn't said much, and Montague hadn't pressed her. After a cup of coffee, she'd seemed to perk up a little, so he'd taken her to a gift shop. That's where he bought the mouse stuffie. It was wearing a t-shirt with a picture of the Eiffel Tower on it. Feeling impulsive, Montague had suggested that they immediately take the stuffie up to the top of the real Eiffel Tower.

They could see it all from up here: the Trocadéro. The Sacré-Cœur. The Arc de Triomphe. It was stunning. But only because he was here with *her*.

"Well?" he asked Daisy, holding her almost as tight as she was holding the stuffie. He couldn't believe how precious she was to him. More precious than his Bentley. More precious than a gold watch. More precious than time itself. "Does the little mouse like it up here?"

"Yes," said Daisy with a long sigh. "We both do."

"You know, we're probably going to have to give that stuffie a name. Could get confusing having *two* little mice."

Daisy giggled. It was good to hear that sound again. "You're right. Hmmm. What's your name, stuffie? Is it something French, like Pierre or Jean-Paul?" She made the mouse shake its head. "No, you're right. I think you're a girl anyway."

"Wait a minute," said Montague, leaning in toward the stuffie. "Do you have something to tell me, mousey?" He put his ear to the stuffie as though it was whispering to him and then said, "Mm-hmm. Yes. I see."

"What did she say?" Daisy asked transfixed, her eyes wide.

"She wonders how you feel about Minnie."

Daisy gasped. "Oh, it's perfect! I love you, Minnie." She cuddled the stuffie, so happy she was almost purring.

Montague stroked her back as they continued to look out at the view of the French capital. "And I love how you don't mind playing with my stuffies in public, Montague. You don't seem embarrassed at all."

Montague held her even tighter. "I could never be embarrassed of you—I'm unbelievably proud. I love that you're comfortable with being who you are in public. It's one of the greatest traits a person can have, in my opinion."

Daisy smiled. "Right back atchya, Daddy."

Montague's heart swelled. After everything they'd been through, it meant so much to him that she still thought of him that way. In spite of himself, he was almost brought to tears. "You know, this is the first time I ever did this."

"You've never been up the Eiffel Tower before?"

"Nope," replied Montague. "Wanted to wait until I had someone special to share the view with. And then I finally found *you*, Minnie," he told the stuffie.

"Hey!" Daisy laughed, giving him a playful push.

"It's Minnie's owner who I'm really into, though," said Montague, bringing the conversation back to sincerity. "Daisy, my sweet little mouse, we haven't known each other that long, but somehow, you've transformed me."

Daisy looked up at him. "I have? Is that a good thing?"

"It's the best thing ever," Montague said. "Because you haven't changed me into someone I'm not. The thing is, you've changed me into who I really am. Who I always was. But I let my bully of a father, my con artist of a wife, and all my stress and fears and baggage get in the way of that. With you, I'm my true self. The self I've always been, deep down."

"That's beautiful," Daisy said, clearly touched. "With you, I feel like I don't have to try all the time."

"You don't have to try?" Montague asked, amused.

"I mean, I don't have to *force* anything. The sunshine is already there. I'm not constantly looking for the bright side, the silver lining. It just...is." Suddenly, Daisy distanced herself from Montague. She held onto her hair which she'd had cut at a Parisian hairdresser this morning. It was quite a bit shorter now, to get rid of the burned bits, but it felt good like that. So much less dry. "But...your wife...Raymond told me about her. And the sexual harassment cases. I guess I've been so tired and in shock since last night I kinda blocked it out." She sighed, long and weary. "I really don't need any more trouble, Montague."

Montague looked at her with his palms spread wide. "I'm so sorry I didn't tell you about Olga sooner," he said. "I've been trying to divorce her for months. Since before my father died." He paused. "She's not a good person. I only married her because she told me she was pregnant. Turns out, it was a lie."

Daisy's jaw dropped. "She lied about being pregnant? Were you devastated? Did you want a baby? Because I'm really not sure if I—"

"I just wanted to do the honorable thing," Montague assured her, then he shook his head. "Worst decision of my life."

"So...what's happening with the divorce? Is it tricky?"

"She's refusing to sign the papers until I give her everything."

"She can't do that!"

Montague shrugged. "Thing is, she *can't* take everything from me. Not unless she somehow takes you."

Daisy smiled, but her smile quickly faded again. "The sexual harassment case..."

"It's not what you think. Turns out, the woman accusing me of that, Penny, was being coerced into lying about it by none other than my lying wife, Olga. The two of them are a couple of coke addicts trying to get my money to fuel their addiction."

"How do you know all this?"

Montague smiled. "I met with them. And I recorded the whole thing. I sent the recording to my lawyer and everything's all worked out."

"Worked out how?"

"I now have proof that I was coerced into the marriage through lies. We're getting the whole thing voided."

"Wow," said Daisy, her eyes shining. "That's great news. So, it's all over?

The marriage, the harassment lawsuit?"

"Not quite, but it will be soon," says Montague. "Give it a few more weeks, and I'll be a free man."

Daisy held Minnie close to her chest. "What about Raymond? Will I ever be free of him?"

Raymond's not gonna be getting out of prison any time soon. But I made sure he'll get some top-notch psychiatric help while he's in there. And I booked Olga and Penny into rehab, too. Turns out you can do a lot on an eight-hour plane ride.

Daisy swallowed and nodded. "I guess I knew there was something wrong with Raymond all along," she said. "I was just in denial. Too full of hope that things would work out okay in the end." She looked at her Daddy. "I guess they did work out...?"

Montague put his arm around her, relieved she was letting him close again. "From my point of view, babygirl, they worked out better than I could have imagined. But...how are *you* feeling now? Honest answer?'"

"Like I've been chewed up and spat out in a million little pieces," she replied with a weak smile.

"Oh, dear." He squeezed her arm. "Let's put you back together again." He kissed her tenderly now. No Daddy stuff. No Dom stuff. Just two souls, sharing a precious moment together.

When they finally pulled apart, Daisy sighed. "I still can't believe you came back to France to rescue me. If you hadn't been there..."

"Your friends were on the case. And the police were aware of the situation. Unfortunately, it took a while to gather enough evidence to storm into the hotel room. But thankfully, when he set off the sprinkler system, he gave us the perfect excuse."

"You must have raced back the instant I told Kiera and Peach where I was."

"Of course I did," he replied. "You needed me. And in all honesty, I missed you terribly."

Daisy grinned. "I'm surprised my friends trusted you enough to tell you where I was."

"I got a bit of a telling off from Kiera," Montague replied. "But they soon realized I just wanted to help."

Daisy smiled. "I don't deserve you."

"You don't think you deserve good things because you've been bullied in the past. It's time to build you up again," Montague told her. "From now on, I'm going to make it my mission to make you into the biggest bighead I know."

Daisy squealed. "No thank you, Daddy!"

"I want you to have the best of everything, darling. You might be a mouse, but you're a princess too."

Daisy smiled up at him. "I already *have* the best of everything, Daddy." She gave him a look. A look that made his cock instantly hard.

"You wanna go back to the hotel, babygirl?"

"Yes, Daddy. Yes, I do."

"Guess I'll cancel our lunch reservation at the Jules Verne restaurant then," Montague said with a wry smile. It was an amazing restaurant, right inside the tower itself. But he got the feeling that what they'd be doing instead would be much, much better.

"Yes, you'd better cancel it," Daisy agreed. "I'm not hungry for food right now, Daddy. I'm hungry for...something else."

Montague grinned. "Just promise me one thing."

"Anything, Daddy."

His gaze trailed down her body and then flicked back to her gorgeous blue eyes. "I get to eat *you* first."

A simple hotel room. Not a five-star place. Not the Presidential Suite. Not even a Disney hotel, which he'd at first suggested. Daisy had requested that they stay somewhere cheap and cheerful. No frills, so that they could focus on each other.

Oddly, Montague had never stayed in a place like this. His whole life had been so charmed. A rich father. A bulging bank account. Rarely a problem that couldn't be solved without a wad of cash.

But this place was dirt-cheap, and yet, surprisingly nice. Besides, he had all he needed in this room.

"I have something to tell you," Daisy said quietly, as they sat on the hotel bed in their underwear, the fan whirring quietly above them.

"What is it, sweetheart?" Montague asked, trailing his finger gently down her shoulder.

"I...lied to you. Well, it wasn't a lie exactly. I just hid something about myself."

Montague nodded, urging her to go on.

"I live in a trailer," she told him. "There's no running water, it kind of stinks, and there's a bunch of scary people living around me who I think maybe one day might try to kill me."

Montague gripped her shoulder tightly. "You did nothing wrong by not telling me. That stuff is personal. I hadn't earned the right to know it. But I'm grateful for you telling me now. I'd like to visit your place when we go back, if you'll have me over."

Daisy hesitated. "Seriously? It's not exactly welcoming."

"I want to share my life with you," Montague told her plainly. "That means the whole thing. The good and the bad."

Daisy nodded. "Well, okay. But I'm planning on getting out of that place."

"You bet your ass you are," Montague said. "I'm hauling your stuff outta there the moment we get back."

"You are, are you?" Daisy said teasingly.

Montague shrugged. "You don't have to move in with me, but I *do* have an entire compound full of empty rooms...And of course there's that lovely little princess room you stayed in last time. The first guest to ever stay there, in fact."

"Seriously? Nobody ever stayed in that room before? Why'd you build it?"

"Because as grumpy as I am," Montague said, "I guess I'm kind of a romantic too. Always holding out for my happy ending."

Daisy smiled and bit her lip. "I'd love to live with you. But... it sounds like there's a catch. Don't tell me...I have to sleep with you to get the key?"

Montague laughed. "No, actually. You never have to do anything you don't want to do."

Daisy lay back on the bed. "Who said anything about don't want to...?"

Montague looked down at her. His PA. His sweetheart. His Forever Girl.

"You know what?" he said. "I'd like to wait until my divorce is granted before I claim you. Until then, I'm afraid it's just going to be weeks and weeks of teasing."

Daisy stuck out her tongue.

"Oh dear," said Montague, tickling her tummy. "That's not what tongues are for, Little girl."

Daisy fluttered her lashes. "What are tongues for, Daddy?"

"Well," he said, "they're for talking....and they're for kissing."

"Sounds rude, Daddy."

"It's actually quite beautiful." He pulled down her white panties, then looked at her pussy. He'd waited so long to kiss this perfect thing, and he was going to enjoy every moment of it. He dipped his head between her legs, running his tongue up and down her inner thighs, then kissing her labia, and her clit.

She gasped. No longer the gasp of a Little girl—in this moment, Daisy was all woman.

He pushed his tongue between her lips, seeking out her clit, delighted at how responsive she was. Trembling legs, moans, arched back. She wanted more so he gave it to her. Flicks. Circles. Pulses.

His fingers wanted in on the action, too. Wanted to find as many ways to pleasure her as possible. He slid two digits inside her pussy while his tongue worked its magic on her clit. She felt so warm and smooth and compact in there. He moved his fingers in a beckoning motion, looking for the G-spot, not willing to back down until he found it.

It didn't take long. Her legs bucked and her hips jerked the moment he found it. He kept up with that beckoning motion, stroking her and loving her as well as he possibly could, completely devoted to his sweet princess.

She rocked and shivered and shook, and at one point, her thighs damn near squeezed his head off, but a moment later, her muscles began to spasm and he knew he had pushed her over the edge.

Beautiful.

He pulled out his fingers, slick with her juices, and moved them round to the back passage now. He sought out her tight rosebud, ready to do it all again but from the opposite way in.

"Bibbity-bob—wait." She sighed. "I don't know about this. Your fingers up there."

"All right, darling," he told her soothingly. "However you like it. You're in charge."

She stroked his hair. "I mean, I always wanted to try it. I'm just nervous in case you don't like it..."

"In case *I* don't like it?"

"Mm-hmm."

"Believe me, sweetheart, I like touching you *everywhere*. But we can try it another time if you like. It's your decision."

"All right," she said, taking a deep breath. "I want to do it with you. But maybe not yet."

"Guess I'll just have to make you come again the old-fashioned way, then..." he told her.

"Sex?" she asked, grinning.

"You wish," he replied, standing up and lying on top of her, sliding his hand into her bra and fondling her nipple with one hand, and strumming her clit with the other.

"I'm not sure if I'll be able to...so soon after..."

She *would*. He knew it. If he wanted to, he could make her come all night long. And someday, he intended to try it.

Right now, though, he backed off a moment, kissing her softly on the lips, knowing how much she'd been through. How important it was that they took things at *her* pace.

She surprised him by grabbing hold of his hand and sliding it back between her thighs. "Don't stop," she whispered.

So he didn't. He worked that hungry little nub of hers again and again, eliciting a whole range of noises from her, until finally, hours later, they fell into a deep sleep together, dreaming of the ocean of orgasms that they had yet to come.

CHAPTER 21 – DAISY

The sun was out.

Daisy hadn't stopped all week. She'd had to give evidence at the police station for what had happened with Raymond. She'd typed up her thoughts on Disneyland Paris for the DDlg theme park Montague was planning. She'd done a bunch of training with Linda, and now she felt much more confident about how to carry out her PA role most effectively. She'd done every single thing Montague had asked for...

Including wearing the love eggs all week.

Of course, she had been extremely professional about it. She'd locked herself in the bathroom every time she'd needed to come. She'd bitten down on her lip and ground her ass down into chairs and done everything she possibly could to release the sexual tension raging within her body without getting caught. She'd even managed to disclose her relationship with Montague to Sam from HR the other day while wearing her love eggs.

Luckily, Sam had no idea. He'd told her that it was fine for the two of them to have a relationship as long as they both consented to it and both kept it professional.

Daisy had nodded, biting her lip, thinking about how good Montague's lips had felt on her pussy. Then, just seconds afterward, with the love eggs rattling around her, she'd run off to the bathroom to make herself come.

Montague had instructed her to keep wearing the eggs daily until he told her otherwise. Each day, she'd come into work, desperate for his next instruction, but it hadn't come.

Montague had been so busy with his lawyer and with catching up on work that there had barely been a moment for the two of them to make eye contact, let alone to touch.

Plus, it had poured down for days and everyone had just sort of...kept their heads down.

Maybe it just hadn't felt like the week for romance for Montague.

But now, finally, it was Friday afternoon, and the sun had started to shine.

"What are you looking at, young lady?"

Daisy startled at Montague's voice behind her. She was standing in his office, looking out of his big window after dropping off a pile of papers on his desk. Then, she'd gotten distracted by the amazing view, as always.

"Sorry, sir," she said. "I just couldn't help admiring the god rays."

Montague stepped beside her and cast her a sideways glance. He looked so good today that it was almost unreal. He'd had his salt and pepper hair cut by the office barber yesterday. His suit, which normally looked a severe and stormy shade of blue, seemed bluer in today's light. More like *lapis lazuli*, or a kingfisher.

"God rays?" Montague asked, looking out the window.

"You know," she said, grinning. "Sunbeams!"

He frowned. "Oh. You mean crepuscular rays."

Daisy laughed. "Cre-*what*?"

"Light from the rising or setting sun passing through particles in the atmosphere and causing beams of light to appear on the horizon."

"Um. I'll stick with god rays, thanks."

Montague nodded. "God rays it is." He turned to Daisy. "I'm sorry I haven't seen much of you this week. Has the hotel been comfortable?"

Montague had been paying for Daisy to stay in a hotel near work. He told her that he couldn't let her stay another night at her old place, but he wanted to help her move into his place properly, on a week that was less hectic for them both. She got that, and she had been extremely grateful for the hotel. Not a laughing man within earshot. She had her special pillowcase with her too, so it felt like home. Plus there was a pool, so who'd turn down an offer like that?

"Yes," Daisy told him. "But I'd really like to collect my stuff from the trailer soon. I want out of that place for good."

"How about tonight?" Montague asked her.

CHAPTER 21 – DAISY

"Really? You have the night off?"

"Uh-huh," said Montague. What was that look? He was almost...smirking. Was he hiding something?

"What does that face mean?" she asked him. "Do you have something fun planned?"

"It's Friday night," Montague told her. "We should *always* have something fun planned on Friday nights."

"Good point," Daisy replied, trying to hide her excitement. "So, we'll go pick up my stuff and then...what? Soft play? Trampolining? Ooh! Mini golf?"

"Anything you like," Montague replied. "I'm in a very good mood, so I'm going to let you pick anything you want in the whole world."

"Wow. That *is* a good mood."

Montague put his arms around her waist, and she sneaked a look back at rest of the office. It was thankfully empty, since it was after four o'clock on a Friday afternoon. That was another of Montague's new rules: everyone finishes early on a Friday. "Daisy," he said to her, "I just found out my marriage has been voided."

Daisy's jaw hit the floor. "You're kidding me. Really? I thought it was going to take weeks."

"Helps if you know the right people."

"Oh my goodness!" Daisy started jumping up and down. "We should celebrate!"

Montague steadied her. "Only if you're in the mood," he replied. "You've been through a lot lately, babygirl. It's only five days since we got back."

"You've been giving me space, Daddy, and I appreciate that," said Daisy, "but I'm ready for things to be... *spaceless* now. If you know what I mean."

He grinned. "Crazy golf it is!"

"No, Daddy," she said quietly.

The way she stressed that word, she hoped he got what she meant.

His eyes trailed down her body. "You want to head straight back to my place?"

Daisy shrugged. "We could always..." She looked around the empty office.

His expression changed. "You're full of surprises, Little one."

"I guess I get impatient like you sometimes," she said. "And these love eggs you've been making me wear all week..."

Montague leaned forward and growled in her ear. "Did you come while you were wearing them?"

She blushed and nodded. "Um. Yup. A few times."

Montague tutted softly. "Oh dear. My Little girl must be very, very horny right now."

She swallowed. "I am, Daddy. It's very difficult to carry on with normal tasks when I'm so... egged up."

Montague smiled, pressing his finger gently against Daisy's lips, then pushing it into her mouth right up to the knuckle.

She sucked on it, remembering how good it felt to have his cock in her mouth...

But then he removed it. "It's very, very naughty of you to have suggested having sex with Daddy at work," he said. "I should spank your little ass for suggesting something so bad. It puts all kinds of bad thoughts in Daddy's head." He trailed his wet finger inside her blouse now, then rubbed it over Daisy's nipple, making it instantly erect.

"Sorry, Daddy," she said quietly.

He took her by the shoulders and directed her gently toward the window. "How about you take a closer look at those god rays, babygirl?"

Daisy swallowed, looking over at the window and then back at her boss. "Yes, sir," she said, pushing her spectacles farther up the bridge of her nose. Then, she stepped right up to the window and placed her palms onto the glass, feeling instantly very naughty indeed to be smearing the perfectly clean surface. She looked back at her boss.

"Take off your skirt and pantyhose," he instructed her. His voice was calm, measured, and authoritative. This was the first time that he'd dominated her since all the stuff with Raymond had happened. She'd told him about what he'd done to her, and he'd rightly figured that she needed a little time to heal. But now, she needed the opposite of a break. She needed to be put together.

Over and over again...

Obediently, Daisy slipped off her shoes and removed the clothing on her lower half. They were so high up here, but she wondered if anyone down on the street could see her. She wasn't necessarily an exhibitionist, but even so, she kind of liked the idea. She was far enough away to feel safe, but it was titillating all the same. She wondered, too, if anyone from the office might still be here, might walk past and see her. But she trusted Montague. He wouldn't do this if there was any risk. She knew that he would look out for her, now and forever.

"Put your shoes back on," he told her. "I like the way your ass looks in them. And bend over."

She did as she was told, then placed her palms back on the glass, sticking her tush right out at him.

"Mmm," he said behind her. "Very nice." He paused. "But that doesn't mean you get away with not having your punishment."

"Uh oh," Daisy said, hiding her smile.

She heard Montague walk up close behind her and shivered with anticipation.

"Fifteen smacks," he whispered into her ear. "One for every day I've known you, you naughty little minx. Turning Daddy's life upside down. Encouraging him to fuck you in the office. Making him hard each and every day for fifteen days, desperate to slide his cock into you."

Daisy was already dripping wet listening to him talk like this. She felt her palms growing sweaty from all the adrenaline coursing around her body.

"Don't forget your safeword," Montague growled into her ear. Then, she felt his strong hand squeeze her buttock.

Pain. But good pain. He was preparing her for what was to come.

The squeezing stopped, but then she felt the first smack.

Immediately, her pussy began to throb with desire. The love eggs rattled around inside her, causing ripples of pleasure all over her groin, her back, her thighs.

"This one's for making Daddy's cock hard in the meeting room," he said, right before he spanked her again.

She cried out in both pain and pleasure. Was it possible to come like this?

"And this one's for making Daddy need to jerk off in the stationery cupboard."

Another slap. More pain. More pleasure.

"Here's one for making Daddy hard on the airplane."

She gasped as her pussy throbbed, aching to be fucked, aching to come.

"And another for giving me a hard-on right at the top of the Eiffel Tower."

The smacks continued to rain down on her, thick and fast. She'd had no idea how often she'd been giving her Daddy hard-ons. And how desperate he'd been to fuck her.

"Daddy," she moaned. "The love eggs...I think I might..."

Montague didn't stop. The spanks felt good and merciless. The kind of spanks that she knew would leave red handprints on her ass for at least a couple days. She'd probably have trouble sitting down, too. She got the feeling there wouldn't be much sitting this weekend anyway...

"And this last one," he told her, "is for making me hard as hell right now."

He spanked her harder than all the other spanks put together, then squeezed her buttocks in his hand. The pain seared through her like a promise.

I promise to fuck you even harder than I just spanked you.

Her legs began to tremble with excitement. Her pussy began to twitch. Her body began to tremor.

"Oh no, I'm..."

She *was*. She was actually coming from being spanked.

Her palms left smeary handprints on the window as she struggled to steady herself. Her pussy dribbled its juices down her inner thigh.

"Well, that's interesting," said Montague, up close behind her. "Looks like we're going to need to work on your self-control."

"No, Daddy," she panted. "I don't want to control myself around you. I want to...let go."

She might have come once, but she was ready for whatever was about to come next. Oh, so ready.

CHAPTER 21 – DAISY

He turned her around, looking deep into her eyes. "Unfortunately, spanking you has made Daddy's cock so hard that he's going to have to fuck you now, princess. Right here at work. So, we're going to have to work on your self-control later."

"Yes, sir," Daisy whispered. "Please, sir."

Montague took off Daisy's blouse and bra then he lifted her, naked, in his arms, cradling her close to his body like she weighed nothing. Her shoes fell to the floor, but he didn't stop to pick them up. All that she had on now was her glasses. All those years of feeling embarrassed by her spectacles, of getting called "four-eyes" and "bug eyes" and "nerd" as a kid, and now, here she was, with her billionaire boss who somehow seemed to find them sexy on her.

Montague carried Daisy out of his office and down the corridor.

"Where are we going?" she asked.

"The meeting room," he said. "I want to spread you out on that nice, big table."

"The meeting room seems fitting," Daisy said with a smile. "A good place for our souls to meet."

"Nobody said anything about our souls," Montague said. "I wanna meet your pussy with my dick, babygirl."

He was being a little crass on purpose, but Daisy still found it sexy. "Plenty of time for our souls to meet later," she joked.

"Sweetheart," he said as he laid her down on the table. "My soul's already fallen deep into yours. As deep as a soul can go."

Daisy looked up at him. "Same here, Daddy."

Montague began loosening his tie and unbuttoning his shirt. She'd dreamed about the two of them doing something like this ever since she'd started working here. Now, it was finally happening. Her powerful boss was undressing for her.

He took off his shirt and Daisy felt her pussy dribble again. She'd seen him topless before, of course, but seeing him here, under the meeting room lights, was something else. Every contour, every muscle, was picked out so sharply. She even loved that smattering of gray hairs on his chest. She loved that he was

179

a real man. Older. Wiser. Sexier than any man she'd ever known.

Now, he began unbuttoning his pants.

"Oh, wait," he said, grabbing something out his pocket. A small, square packet. Durex. She couldn't help noticing the light blue packet. She'd seen those at the pharmacy before: size XXL. "I'm clean," he told her. "Got tested after Olga. And there's been nobody since. But—"

"I'm clean too," said Daisy. "Raymond made me test before the wedding. And after that we never..."

"Up to you, babygirl," he said. "You on contraception?"

Daisy nodded shyly. "IUD."

"Happy to wear it if you want."

Daisy shook her head. "No, Daddy. I want to feel you. As long as we're exclusive—"

"Sweetheart," Montague said, looking down at her. "We're beyond exclusive. It's me and you for as long as you'll have me. You're my Forever Girl."

Daisy giggled. "And you're my Forever Daddy."

Montague took down his pants in one swift movement, revealing his designer boxers and the huge bulge in them underneath.

He paused a moment, looking at Daisy's pussy, and then he let out a long, low growl. "Damn, I'm gonna enjoy this. Just let me know if your ass starts to hurt too much on that table, okay?"

"I think I'm going to like it that way, sir," Daisy said submissively.

"Good." Montague pulled down his boxers, his thick cock springing out of them, slapping gently against his toned stomach. Yup. He really was an XXL. Daisy had never seen anything like it. Montague's made Raymond's look like a kid's crayon.

Daisy opened her legs a little wider, giving him a good look at her.

He smiled appreciatively, stroking his cock a couple times as he took her in. "You know, that thing is a work of fucking art, baby."

Daisy wasn't sure how he could find the look of her pussy so enticing. To her, it just looked like little flaps of skin and a hole. But it definitely seemed to do something to him. His cock grew even longer, even wider.

Montague put his fingers near her pussy, and then she felt him pulling the love eggs out of her, slick with her juices. She gasped at the sensation, feeling close to climaxing again.

"Don't you dare come until Daddy's cock is inside you," he ordered her.

"Sorry, Daddy," she whispered. "I'll be good."

He climbed onto the heavy oak meeting table now, his body poised over hers, his mouth on her lips. He kissed her long and deep, his cock nudging between her legs as he did so, desperate to find its own way up there.

She was so wet already that she wondered if he'd just slip in.

Clearly, though, Montague was enjoying taking his time. He pulled away from her lips, and his kisses trailed down her neck, her clavicle, her breastbone, her breasts, her stomach.

"I've never wanted to fuck anyone so damn much," he said, grabbing his cock and positioning herself over her.

She shivered at the sight of him. So erect. So primal. So hungry for her.

"Time for me to claim you, Little one," he said, pumping his cock a couple times and then pushing it down between her thighs.

Instantly, she felt the engorged tip, nudging at her entrance. It felt so good that her pussy flooded immediately and she swallowed him in. With his smooth, bulbous tip inside of her, she already felt so opened up that she wondered if she could come just like this. But there was more.

His cock slid into her now and it just seemed to keep on going. More and more of it, deeper and deeper, like a train going through a never-ending tunnel. Eventually, though, it did end, squashing up against her cervix like it could have kept on going if it hadn't been for the barrier. Like it could have grown and grown for all eternity, just for her.

"Holy fuck, girl," Montague breathed into her ear. "You *are* my fairy fucking godmother."

Daisy moaned with pleasure. "You feel amazing too, sir. Daddy. Boss."

"Call me whatever the hell you like, babygirl," he said. "As long as you call me yours."

He moved inside of her now. Sliding in and out in the way both their bodies were designed to do. In and out. Making each other moan and gasp and shake.

Daisy's ass felt sore against the hard table, but it wasn't an unpleasant sensation. Rather, it was a stinging reminder that she was his. She gripped onto him with her legs, allowing his cock to get deeper. She could hardly believe that his thick shaft was able to penetrate her so freely. He was stretching her open, filling every crevice within her most intimate passage, and yet it felt perfectly natural. Perfectly right.

The more that he fucked her, the more that her brain started to switch off. She found her body becoming nothing more than a bundle of sensations, a tangle of desire for him.

"Daddy…" she moaned. "My butt…"

"Your butt hurts too much?" he panted, slowing down.

"No," she gasped, shaking her head. "Your finger. My butt."

He knew exactly what she wanted, and he gave it to her. He bit down on her shoulder as he started to insert his finger into her asshole. As he did so, he fucked her harder and harder. Bucking and biting and fingering her bum on the boardroom table.

The table she would have to sit at on Monday morning and pretend like this never happened. The table that she would be thinking about for the rest of her days.

"Fuck," moaned Montague. "I'm close. Touch your clit."

She did immediately and obediently.

He moved his finger in and out of her asshole as he thrust inside of her. His finger knew exactly what to do, exactly how to find her G-spot from this new angle, to bring her over the edge with him. He moved faster now. The table started to rock beneath them. Would they break it? Montague didn't seem to care, so she didn't either. She let herself be carried upstream by him, lifted higher and higher and higher until they reached the top of a cliff, and then—

Then, they leaped over the edge in perfect synchronicity, in slow motion with one another, trembling, coming, claiming.

She was full of him now. His cock, his cum, his soul. And it felt like sunshine.

CHAPTER 22 – MONTAGUE

"So, this is where my sweet little thing grew up, huh?"

Daisy nodded. "Well, not in this exact ice cream bar. Back when I lived here, I think this was a hair salon. Otherwise, I'd have been here, like, every day."

Montague smiled. "I like the whole area. It's very..."

What's a polite word for it?

"Suburby?" Daisy hazarded, grinning.

"Yes," said Montague. Putting on a funny voice, he said: "If you like suburbia, you'll love this place."

"It's true," said Daisy, laughing. "Nothing wrong with it. It's just kind of... meh. I like being on the coast, but it's all very...calm. Maybe it's good if you have a family and want a bit more space and good schools and stuff like that. But...that's not the life for me. I don't know how my friends have ended up staying here so long—I've wanted out for as long as I can remember. I just always felt like I wanted adventures, you know?"

Montague nodded. "Sure. But it's always nice to have a base to come back to."

"A nice little base like your zillion-dollar compound," joked Daisy.

Montague loved how Daisy had grown more confident about gently teasing him. It helped to have someone like him keeping her in check. And it helped *her* to have someone like him building her up. She had seemed so happy since they'd moved in together. They used the fairy-tale room whenever she was feeling Little. And *his* bedroom, with all of its specialist Dom equipment, when he was feeling...Big.

The Sunshine Trailer Park had been a bit of a shock, though. Nothing sunshiney about that place. It was dangerous and depressing. Seeing where Daisy had lived had made him want to wrap his arms around her and never let her out of his sight. Poor girl. Not even any running water.

That was two weeks ago, though. The day after his visit to the park, he'd gotten on the phone to the guy who owned the place and threatened court action through his lawyer if the guy didn't sort out the plumbing. The owner had been a real asshole. Said he'd be glad if the place got shut down, that it was too much hard work.

So Montague had stepped in. As of last week, he'd become the park's official owner. Since then, he'd found alternative accommodation and medical help for all of its residents. If someone had told Montague three months ago what the accommodation was that he'd found for them, he'd have sworn they were making it up. He'd given them his father's house. It was a genius idea, really. The house was big enough for twenty residents, with beautiful views over Miami Beach, a pool, plenty of luxurious touches. It was the perfect place for people with difficult lives to piece them back together. Plus, Montague couldn't deny that there was a certain pleasure in deciding to give it to the needy. His father would have hated the idea. Well, screw him. This was the one useful thing he'd ever done for the world.

He had big plans for Sunshine Trailer Park, too. Goodbye, shitty old trailers without plumbing. Hello, brand new trailer park specifically for Littles in need of help. A gated community for Littles who had been made homeless, or who were running away from an abusive partner or parent, or who just needed some space for a while. It was all in honor of Daisy, of course. His brave babygirl, who he hoped would never have to suffer again.

"I hope Kiera and Peach get here soon," Daisy grumbled, studying the menu. "If I don't eat some ice cream soon, I think I might just explode."

"Ah, I've heard of that disease," said Montague. "No ice-cream-itis. Very serious."

Just then, the door of the ice cream parlor opened and two young women walked in. One of them looked kinda punky, with cropped black hair and a lip piercing. If it hadn't been for the fact that she was wearing a t-shirt with a picture of Barbie on it, she might have looked badass. The other had pink hair and big brown eyes. She was carrying a little white Shih Tzu that looked like it had *major* attitude.

"Here they are!" squealed Daisy, jumping up on her seat.

Montague cringed as she put her sneakers on the seat. He decided not to embarrass Daisy in front of her friends, but he'd have words with her about treating furniture with respect later.

Daisy hugged her friends, who seemed equally as excitable as she did, and then the three of them—plus the dog—headed over.

"Daddy," said Daisy. "These are my friends." She pointed to the almost badass one. "Kiera." Then, she pointed to the pink-haired one. "And Peach."

"Good to meet you both," said Montague, shaking their hands. "But... aren't you forgetting someone?"

They all looked confused until Montague pointed at the dog.

"Oh!" said Peach, giggling. "This is Teddy. And I chose this venue to meet because it's literally the only ice cream parlor in the neighborhood that lets you bring dogs in."

They all sat in the booth together, including Teddy.

"I'm glad you two have arrived," said Montague. "Daisy has been struggling to figure out which ice cream she wants, so maybe you two can help her."

"Oh man, this is always the hard part," said Kiera. "Do I go for a Butterfinger Sundae, or a Dirty Fisherman?"

"Ew, what's a Dirty Fisherman?" asked Daisy. "I missed that one!"

"Chocolate ice cream, chocolate syrup, and gummy worms," said Kiera.

"Hmmm, Daisy replied. Not so *ew* after all."

"I like the sound of the Snowshoe," said Peach. "Marshmallows and chopped nuts."

"Oh my gosh, that sounds so good," said Daisy. "But I think I'd regret it for the rest of my life if I didn't have the Brownie Sundae!"

She looked over at Montague, fluttering her eyelashes. "Daddy, am I allowed *two* sundaes?"

Peach and Kiera went uncomfortably quiet. For some reason, they were avoiding eye contact with Montague.

"I don't think two is a very good idea," said Montague, reaching out for his Little's hand. "I think you'd regret it if you only picked *two*. Let's get one of everything!"

Peach and Kiera looked up, amazed.

"What?! But that's, like, sixteen flavors!" said Kiera.

"We'll ask for half-portions," said Montague. "And we'll pass them around."

"Wow," Kiera replied. "I'm honestly amazed." She nudged Daisy and hissed: "Raymond would never even let you have *one* ice cream, let alone *sixteen*."

Peach giggled. "You're only allowed one, though, Teddy."

"I'm not sure dogs are allowed ice cream," said Montague. "I draw the line there."

"It's okay," Peach explained. "They do a special doggy ice cream here. Peanut butter and banana, with special doggy cookies crumbled up on top."

"All right," Montague laughed. "Just as long as he eats his on the floor. We don't want it to get mixed up and eat Teddy's ice cream."

Everybody laughed and Montague found himself relaxing a little. He hadn't realized it until now, but he'd been nervous about meeting Daisy's friends. They were so important to her, and it seemed like they'd hated her ex with a passion. He could see why Daisy liked them, though. They had her best interests at heart, just like he did.

"All right, ladies," he said. "I'll leave you to catch up for a minute, and I'll go ask the server about our slightly unconventional request."

Daisy smiled. "Thank you, Daddy."

"You can thank me later," he replied, "when you're in a sugar coma."

As he walked over to the counter, he heard Peach whisper: "I think *I* want a Daddy next. What about you, Kiera?"

"Nah," Kiera replied. "I'm a lone ranger. Although your Daddy seems pretty cool, Daisy."

Montague smiled to himself. He had their stamp of approval. That was good for Daisy. It was good for everyone.

CHAPTER 22 – MONTAGUE

He put in his request to the server for every ice cream on the list.

The server was a little taken aback but willing to fulfill the order. "It might take me a while, though," she said. "Are you good to wait?"

"Definitely," replied Montague, looking back at his girl. "We have all the time in the world."

"I can't believe you're letting us extend the trip!" Daisy squealed, jumping up and down. She had chocolate smeared around her lips, despite his best efforts at wiping it off. He didn't mind, though. She looked cute like that. Plus, it was a reminder of all the fun they'd had.

"How could I refuse?" Montague said. "Kiera wants to show you her new bubble bath collection, and Peach has invited us to Teddy's first dog show."

Daisy was so happy she was practically skipping. "Plus, there's this really fun trampoline place I want to show you!"

Despite their jokes about this place being suburbia, Montague loved how connected to the place she was. He knew she'd had a tough childhood, but he also knew how important it was for her to hold onto the good memories too.

"I want to see it all," he told her. "And now that I know that I've passed the friend test, and that they want to hang out with me again, I'm up for staying all week if you are."

"But, Daddy, what about all your work?"

Montague grinned. It was a big grin. One of *Daisy's* grins. "My work will still be there when I get back."

"That's very naughty of you, Daddy," said Daisy. "I think I'll have to spank your bottom when we get back to the hotel."

For the first time in all his life, Montague let out a big, loud, belly laugh. It shocked them both for a second.

"Woah," said Daisy, after recovering. "That is the best laugh I've ever heard. I hope to hear it again sometime."

"You'll have to keep telling your terrible jokes, then," he said, pinching her hip like a crab claw.

"Hey!" Daisy laughed, pinching him back. Then, suddenly, she stopped. "Wait. This isn't the hotel. You've taken us to the marina."

Montague nodded. "I have a surprise for you."

"We're about to go skinny-dipping?"

Montague laughed that big belly laugh again.

"Wow," said Daisy. "I guess my jokes are getting funnier."

"Look over there," said Montague, guiding her toward the water's edge. Moored on the edge of the ocean was his custom-designed, one-of-a-kind floating mansion. A project that he'd put his heart and soul into, working with architects and builders to get everything just so. Light, bright, contemporary. Timber accents, natural stone elements, breathtaking walls of glass.

"What's that?" Daisy asked. "A house, or a boat?"

"A little bit of both," Montague replied. "I had her brought up here so that you could come stay near your friends any time you wanted. We both can. And if you prefer to lift anchor and go on an adventure sometime, we can do that too."

"But that's...amazing," Daisy replied. "It's so...romantic. Like living in a little cabin, but a cabin that moves."

Montague laughed. "You should check out my actual cabin sometime."

Daisy giggled. "Do you ever think you might just be *too* rich, Daddy?"

"If you want, I'll give it all away," he told her. "As long as I get to keep you."

Daisy looked up at him. "Just promise me you'll never get rid of this houseboat, OK?" She paused. "And I guess I like the compound, too. And I'm quite excited by the sound of this cabin you mentioned..."

He laughed, taking her hand. "Ready to explore?"

"You bet!" she replied.

"Be aware, it's only got two bedrooms," Montague told her. "But I hope you don't mind, I made one of them into a nursery."

Daisy froze. "You're not...you're not saying you want to have kids, are you?"

Montague shook his head. "No, sweetheart. I'm saying I made it into a special room for you. I call it 'A Little House for a Little Mouse.'"

Daisy breathed a sigh of relief and laughed. "Oh good. That sounds amazing. I sure hope there's cheese."

"There's cheese," said Montague. "And there's a big screen to watch the Disney channel on. And there's even a spanking chair if you get too naughty."

"You really have thought of everything, Daddy," said Daisy as they walked toward the boat. "But honestly, I was *kinda* just hoping to spank your bottom tonight and then stuff my face with cheese."

Montague laughed again.

"You know that you're a sunshine person, really?" Daisy told him. "Deep down?"

Montague stopped walking and put his arms around her. "And you know I have you to thank for discovering that?"

Daisy nuzzled into him. "All I know, Daddy," she said, "is that I found you. And that we have a lifetime of discoveries and adventure ahead of us. If that's not a fairy-tale ending, then tell me what is?"

They held hands tightly as they walked together to the water's edge.

"It *is* a fairy-tale ending," Montague assured her. "It's the sunshine after the storm."

* * *

Thanks so much for reading! Don't forget to sign up to my mailing list for exclusive content and updates!

And don't forget Book Two in the Daddies Inc series! Watch Peach and Isaac concoct a business plan that goes very wrong... and then very, very right. Check out YES DADDY on Amazon now!

Plus, find me on Facebook!

And lastly, please review this book on Amazon. Every review means so much to me! :)

Lucky x

ALSO BY THE AUTHOR

BAD BOY DADDIES
DADDY MEANS BUSINESS
DADDY MEANS TROUBLE
DADDY MEANS SUBMISSION
DADDY MEANS DOMINATION
DADDY MEANS HALLOWEEN

LIBERTY LITTLES
TAMED BY HER DADDIES
FAKE DADDY
DADDY SAVES CHRISTMAS (IN A LITTLE COUNTRY
CHRISTMAS)
SECOND CHANCE DADDIES
DADDY'S GAME
THE DADDY CONTEST
DADDY'S ORDERS

DRIFTERS MC
DADDY DEMANDS
DADDY COMMANDS
DADDY DEFENDS

DADDIES INC
BOSS DADDY
YES DADDY

COLORADO DADDIES
HER WILD COLORADO DADDY
FIERCE DADDIES

THE DADDIES MC SERIES
DANE
ROCK
HAWK

DADDIES MOUNTAIN RESCUE
MISTER PROTECTIVE
MISTER DEMANDING
MISTER RELENTLESS

SUGAR DADDY CLUB SERIES
PLATINUM DADDY
CELEBRITY DADDY
DIAMOND DADDY
CHAMPAGNE DADDY

LITTLE RANCH SERIES
DADDY'S FOREVER GIRL
DADDY'S SWEET GIRL
DADDY'S PERFECT GIRL
DADDY'S DARLING GIRL
DADDY'S REBEL GIRL

MOUNTAIN DADDIES SERIES
TRAPPED WITH DADDY
LOST WITH DADDY
SAVED BY DADDY
STUCK WITH DADDY
TRAINED BY DADDY
GUARDED BY DADDY

STANDALONE NOVELS
PLEASE DADDY
DADDY'S PROMISE

DDLG MATCHMAKER SERIES
DADDY'S LITTLE BRIDE
DADDY'S LITTLE REBEL
DADDY'S LITTLE DREAM

LITTLE BEST FRIENDS SERIES
DADDY DOCTOR
DADDY BODYGUARD
DADDY BILLIONAIRE

COPYRIGHT

Content copyright © Lucky Moon. All rights reserved. First published in 2022.

This book may not be reproduced or used in any manner without the express written permission of the copyright holder, except for brief quotations used in reviews or promotions. This book is licensed for your personal use only. Thanks!

Disclaimer: This is a work of fiction. Names, characters, businesses, places, events, locales, and incidents are either the products of the author's imagination or used in a fictitious manner. Any resemblance to actual persons, living or dead, or actual events is purely coincidental.

Cover Image © Dante Dellamore. Cover Design, Lucky Moon.

Printed in Great Britain
by Amazon

21889774R10109